Dedication

I dedicate this novel to my loving parents John (Jack) and Violet (Vi), who had very little in the way of wealth but gifted my sister Teresa and myself a fortune in love and care

If Good Men Do Nothing

Cliff Comber

ISBNs:
Paperback: 978-1-80227-003-7
eBook: 978-1-80227-004-4

Published by PublishingPush.com

Contents

Acknowledgements

My extreme gratitude to the following who have made this final book in the Dennis Dutch French series possible:

Ross Beare the proprietor of Holmbush Paintball, Horsham for allowing me unlimited access to his game sites and imparting his knowledge of all activities available there, local journalist Martin Read for overseeing my work, and for his continuous support over the years, my running adversary (although he was always the victor) retired Regimental Sergeant Major and paratrooper Malcolm 'Mac' French, for supplying the foreword and giving me an insight into military life, Jon Shipway, another former para and lifelong friend who has allowed me to use his character in each novel, Sgt Chris Morley 1PWRR Snipers for his valuable contribution and expert advice. I greatly appreciate the assistance from my good friend Jeff of Jeff Woodall photography for creating the image on the front cover and of the author. At last (but never least!), my thanks to my wife Carla who will be so relieved that, now I have finally put my stories onto paper, I will no longer be hailing for her assistance in fixing my computer errors or answering my spelling requests.

It would be remiss of me not to mention my late friends and colleagues Dennis Chopping and Tony Byrne, who amongst others inspired me to write my novels.

As this is the completion of the Dennis 'Dutch' French trilogy, I wish to thank all my friends and relatives, especially Michelle Page, who have supported this 'wannabe' author, and of course my gratitude goes out to all those who have taken the time to read and review my words.

Foreword

I was born in York but most definitely made in the British army. Honed by the Parachute Regiment which I served a total of 23 years, seeing many parts of the world and involved in different conflicts I learned how to plan extensively both in training and operational scenarios. This, linked with my strong disciplinarian views and self-belief, undoubtedly helped me achieve some of the high accolades of my life.

From my own humble background and vast military experience, I can whole heartedly identify with both the character and motives of 'Dutch French' and hope you enjoy his daring and explosive exploits in this and the two previous novels.

Malcolm French
Warrant Class One
Regimental Sergeant Major(retired)
Now residing with those hills/
mountains/lakes of Cumbria
September 2020

Rear cover photograph : Malcolm French leading the way up the slopes of Pen y Fan, Brecon Beacons.

The loveliest spot that man hath found.
William Wordsworth

You may leave the Lake District, but once you've been, it'll never leave you.

Anonymous

Prologue

A deadly dispute between retired soldier Dennis 'Dutch' French and an Eastern European-led criminal gang had originated some three years before, following the rape of French's wife Melanie on the Sussex Downs, on the outskirts of Brighton. Due to this attack and her two previous miscarriages, Melanie had been left both mentally and physically damaged and subsequently refused to assist in any further criminal investigation, or any possible court proceedings should her assailants be discovered.

Devastated by the damage caused to Melanie, her husband, keen to seek justice carried out his own investigation, tracing the two Eastern European car cleaners responsible as they were about to inflict an almost identical crime on another woman. Dutch, by chance, interrupted their assault, shooting both men dead with a trophy gun that he had smuggled into the U.K whilst in the army. During this altercation he gained confirmation that Melanie's ordeal had been filmed by the two now deceased men and learnt that the images were in possession of the manager of a car valeting depot in Lewes, Sussex, where the two attackers were employed. This was one of a chain of similarly organised businesses run by a large and vicious international criminal cartel, mainly situated in the south of England.

Following forward planning and surveillance, Dutch, a very skilled, decorated, and resourceful ex paratrooper, again decided to take the law into his own hands, to destroy the film of his wife's dreadful ordeal in any manner possible.

His observations enabled him to trap the manager concerned, together with two other leading members of the gang inside a portacabin, where he believed the images of his wife were contained. Just prior to setting the portacabin alight he was surprised to be joined by a former aggrieved member of the car cleaning work force, Jorge.

Jorge, an illegal immigrant who had recently been assaulted by one of the three inside of the cabin, equally blamed each of three incarcerated men for the death of his sister, also an illegal immigrant, who had been forced by the gang into a life of drugs and prostitution, resulting in her taking her own life. The subsequent fire was started by both men and the inferno quickly disposed of all three gang members, also destroying any film once contained in the makeshift office.

Dutch and Jorge made good their exit and parted shortly afterwards, when Jorge boarded a train to Newcastle where his brother resided.

Dutch was aware that the police would possibly connect him with the five deaths. Although confident that he had meticulously covered his tracks by not leaving any forensic evidence at either scene, he felt it was necessary to temporarily leave the country, should any evidence be forthcoming. As part of his forward planning he had made arrangements for Melanie and himself to travel to Venezuela for work, as this was a country that had no extradition arrangement with the U.K, should he become an officially wanted person.

Both Melanie, and Dutch worked in different roles for an oil executive and lived happily, in privileged conditions compared with most of the country's population who were undergoing economic upheaval. During an attempt to kidnap the executive, Dutch, who was employed as personal security guard, once again came close to death, and the nine lives that he believed that he once possessed had now well and truly expired. The attack resulted in a change in the conditions of Melanie's employment, which subsequently caused her to return home. Dutch in an effort to complete the terms of his working contract remained, but a concerned message from his wife encouraged him to return to the U.K urgently.

As he was a possibly a wanted person he was forced to travel illegally under a false identity. Once on home soil he went about executing a plan to illuminate the threat to which Melanie had alerted him.

His meticulously planned scheme resulted in the two would be assassins being shot and killed by an equally murderous duo.

Shortly after the elimination of his pursuers, Dutch together with Melanie, her parents Molly and Ken, and their beloved dog Jodie moved their home to the Lake District. Having settled into their new surroundings and commencing his own business, Dutch decided that the time was right to make himself available to be interviewed by the police. Although it was gamble that the police had insufficient evidence to connect him to any of the seven deaths, he felt that it was a chance that he had to take in order to lead a normal and straightforward life. Following his arrest and formal interview he was released from custody due to the lack of evidence.

After three long years he was now able to put all threats behind him, and to live both anonymously and peacefully, with his wife and her parents in a distant part of the country.

But such relaxing thoughts soon diminished when he received a visit from two gang members who informed him in no uncertain terms that he had only survived because a suitable opportunity to eliminate him had not arisen.

The continuing and unexpected threat left Dutch unnerved, not knowing where and when the gang would try again.

"The only thing necessary for the triumph of evil is for good men do nothing".
Edmund Burke

CHAPTER 1

In the Country *(1966)*

Artists: Cliff Richard and The Shadows
Writers: Bennett, Marvin, Rostill, Welch

Dennis, like so many others found solace within the beauty of the lakes and its surrounding countryside. Each season took on a new vista, seemingly removing him far away from normal everyday problems, which was further enhanced by his settled family life and successful business. As a youngster from a deprived background and subjected to bullying his escape from unpleasant situations had been listening to music which had developed into a habit of associating song titles to certain situations, a practice that had continued into adult life. He had noticed that since his move the tunes to which he was choosing to listen had taken on a more joyful and optimistic note.

Although only having resided in the area for a short time he already knew that this part of Cumbria was the place that he would spend the rest of his life. Such peace and tranquillity had not come about without many problems for Dennis 'Dutch' French, who had, until recent events, thought that this was a turning point in his life.

Several months of normality had passed since the unexpected hostile visit from two members of the aggrieved cartel. Dutch remained both shocked and puzzled as to how the foreign led gang had discovered his move from the South Coast to the Lake District so quickly, despite his meticulous planning by only revealing his real name and address to limited sources.

Amongst the trusted few were the Army pension office, HM Revenue and Customs and his new doctor and dentist practices, as he was aware that these organisations required up to date information which they should not disclose without his specific authority. All of his other necessary correspondence was sent to a PO box at his local sorting office, and in an effort for all to remain safe, exactly the same procedures were practiced by both his wife and in-laws.

As secure as he thought their anonymity was, he was unaware that the aggrieved cartel had an informant in a central administration role in the National Health Service who had access to the medical records of the entire population. Under duress this employee was providing regular information to the criminal gang and was soon able to answer their request for an up-date, by supplying details of a recent transfer of address for a Dennis French formerly from Brighton to Cumbria. The same NHS employee had informed gang member Yannis Stanescu of the address where Melanie was living following her brutal rape and assault. Stanescu, together with a colleague, visited the address with a view to avenging the death of his brother Ivan, by killing her husband Dennis, the chief suspect. But French had turned the tables on the two potential assassins, who through his intricate deceit, were both shot dead by two equally vicious brothers.

This episode had persuaded him to make the 330 miles move North, to commence his own business as a private mini-bus tour operator and to eventually surrender himself to the police for questioning regarding the deaths of all seven cartel members. Due to his interest and knowledge of forensic science, the police had been unable to locate sufficient evidence at either of the scenes to connect him to any of the deaths and he was subsequently released without charge.

The unwelcomed villains left him in no doubt that although they had not been afforded the opportunity to deal with him on the day of their visit, they would return at a later date to finish the job. As they had unnecessarily revealed themselves and their intentions, the impending threat was to make him sweat, not knowing where and when they would next strike.

This threat had forced Dutch to step up his already stringent counter-surveillance methods. Although he had little remorse regarding his hasty and unconventional actions taken against his tormentors, he heavily regretted the unnecessary anxiety and upheaval that he had caused his family, placing them all in imminent danger. Not wishing to further concern his wife and her ageing parents, he had not informed them that he had been traced and the threat on his life had resumed. Such devastating news would shatter their new idyllic and settled lifestyles. Even before the impromptu threatening visit, Dutch had previously been warned that this particularly large criminal organisation had a reputation of tracing and severely punishing anyone that transgressed against them. With this in mind, since his move to the town of Ambleside with its 2,600 population, he had meticulously parked his sixteen- seater Mercedes tour bus in a secure barn situated on a farm, only a short cycle ride from the home that he now shared with his wife and his in-laws. He carried out this practice so that the distinctive blue and green vehicle, logoed 'Lucky's Lakeland Tours' with a four leaf clover pictured on the bonnet, would not be easily connected to his home address. But, since the cartel had now traced him, he doubted whether this practice, or the diversion of mail and all of his other methods to elude them, remained effective. Having come to terms with this concern, he would now have to be even more vigilant. Although the attempt on his life could arise at any time, he was fairly confident that it would be by way of an ambush in quiet surroundings, as they had already inferred that their most recent plans were disrupted as they had not been afforded the perfect opportunity. He further thought that they would perhaps not consider approaching his home as they might believe that he would be prepared and still in possession of the Walther pistol used to eliminate the pair that had raped his wife. But the potential assailants were unaware that he was now unarmed, as in an effort to evade detection he had dismantled and disposed of the weapon in a tidal river. To detect any possible intruders on his property, he immediately obtained four ground movement detectors that had served him so well in the past. He was able to monitor them from a small transistor radio without alarming or alerting Melanie to the recent threat, as she was familiar with his use of the devices and knew that he had always been a vigilant and crime conscious individual.

CHAPTER 2

Let's Work Together *(1970)*

Artists: Canned Heat
Writer: Wilbert Harrison

As the summer months proceeded, the Lakeland country-side was a mass of colourful beauty, attracting attendance from all over the globe. With so many visitors to the area, Dutch decided to take a tour of the district to visit the commercial premises that supported his business, both to renew acquaintances, and, if necessary replenish, his advertising leaflets. When doing so, wherever possible he would speak to the owners or managers of the establishments. In the main such visits were to cafes, shops, pubs, and hotels, all of which received a commission for any business generated.

Whilst on route to a large outlying country hotel, he saw a sign at the entrance to a large farm site. The multi coloured paint splattered notice read 'Paintball' which included a telephone number and a directional arrow. Dutch had seen the sign before and had considered suggesting to some of the runners from the athletic club that he had recently joined that they should spend a day at the facility. It suddenly occurred to him that active and adventurous visitors holidaying in the area might well visit the facility, making this business another ideal place to promote his own company.

Without further hesitation he turned onto the narrow concrete road that led to the farm. He continued to drive between the farm buildings, which included a large haybarn and as he did so he was surprised to see how many other small commercial premises were situated there. Amongst those easily visible were a mechanical workshop, a small cafe and farm shop, an event catering office, a Koi fish shop and two large buildings accommodating different removal companies.

Apart from various commercial lorries and vans there were a number of vehicles, including two extremely battered, mud- splattered Land Rovers, that looked only fit for off road use. A signpost indicated further units situated in a courtyard at the rear of the buildings.

Dutch stopped opposite the 4X4 vehicles adjacent to a very large windowless blue corrugated metal panel-built barn. The only visible entrance was by two big, heavy solid metal doors, which were closed together and secured by a purposely constructed metal shield, which partially concealed a heavy security padlock. Dutch was able to read a cardboard notice attached to the doors, on which was printed,

"Out on site at present. If you need to contact me call the below mobile number or follow the signs to find me. Ross."

Being keen to both further his business contacts and to view the site for a possible future visit, Dutch followed the directional arrows, turning onto a tarmac track that ran alongside a wood fencing company and an agricultural machinery workshop. Dutch was amazed at how many businesses were situated in such a remote area and considered that perhaps it was because such premises were far cheaper to rent there, rather than in a more populated location. The solid road concluded in front of a large detached house, to the left of which was a single lane track controlled by an open metal security gate with a heavy security chain wrapped around its frame. Also situated at the entrance, opposite the gate was an information board with a wooden box attached containing brochures about the sporting facility and a further instruction notice to keep all windows closed. Dutch then drove through the entrance, continuing to follow the directional arrows along a mixed stone and broken brick track. He carefully weaved his way along the track avoiding as many ruts and long-standing puddles in order to keep his pristine vehicle as clean as possible. After passing sparse scrub on his left in which numerous wooden barricades could be seen, he came across a long abandoned overturned saloon car. Dutch continued to follow the signs until the path on which he was travelling reached a further track to his left. Two printed signs with arrows at the junction indicating that the 'Ultimate Events Activity Centre' was straight ahead, following the track into a tall pine forest through an identical metal gate that he had previously negotiated. The second sign showed 'Paintball Centre' to the left. As he completed the left-hand turn, he was surprised at what confronted him. The first objects to gain his attention positioned on a grass bank was a monstrous gunmetal grey missile, approximately 20 feet in length accompanied by three warheads all covered by camouflaged cargo netting, with a rocket launching cannon situated nearby. A sign opposite a log-built sentry hut indicated 'Border Checkpoint' where entry could be controlled by the presence of the fixed heavy metal raised security pole. Ominously, overlooking the checkpoint was an enclosed camouflaged painted armoured machine gun nest. Continuing, he could see through the tall bracken and rhododendron bushes further numerous crudely built wooden barricades on either side of the track, encompassed by raised black nylon netting, protecting any users of the lane from stray missiles.

Dutch then drove onto an extensive stone surface clearing capable of accommodating many parked cars.

Much of the clearing was surrounded by high grassed banking interspersed with tall pine trees and further rhododendron bushes and bracken, all shrouded with safety netting. His attention was then drawn to a large log constructed fort. With its large wooden doubled hinged gates and 15-foot-high walls, it represented to Dutch his impression of what wild west forts such as Fort Laramie, Fort Apache or the Alamo might have looked like, once read about in comics as a youngster. He was intrigued by the structure and for a moment forgot the purpose of his visit, just wishing to explore what he considered to be an area of great interest.

After parking next to yet another distressed looking 4x4, he approached the impressive building, noticing that to the left of the Fort was a stretched caravan and two metal cargo containers. On the opposite side of the Fort another identical container formed part of the log wall, all of which were painted in camouflaged brown and green. As Dutch passed under the large 'Welcome' sign positioned between the two watch towers situated either side of the gates, to which a large Rules sign was attached, he entered a partially roofed area. Within this space there were dozens of wooden tables and benches with a sign indicating free tea and coffee. Among the other designated facilities was a check in counter, combat clothing store, paint office displaying prices for paintballs, grenades and additional armoury, and a large blackboard for adding and subtracting scores for specific tasks. There were further notices at entrances to the gaming areas, reminding participants to wear googles.

As Dutch walked through the building, he heard the sound of hammering coming from outside. Having seen the sign for the viewing tower he climbed the steps onto a wooden two-tier roofed construction which was enclosed in wire mesh fencing and reinforced with fine black plastic protective netting. As he looked out onto the 'war game' site, he could see a man dressed in a red hooded sweatshirt hammering large stakes into the ground. The man was at the far end of a mud and grass field which partially resembled a World War One battleground with trenches, machine gun emplacements and further numerous white painted, roughly built wooden barricades scattered around. At one end of the battlefield there was a large replica wooden house, with a realistic looking castle and church situated directly opposite on the other side of the field. Through the open castle door, he noticed that there were stairs leading to the turret. Having been sniper-trained he couldn't help thinking about what a temporary advantageous position this would be until the arrival of any opposition heavy artillery.

Dutch was very impressed with what he considered was an extremely professional set up and could imagine that all participants would very much enjoy the experience there.

He waited until the lone man finished his task and then shouted, "Excuse me, can I come down and talk to you?"

The man wiping his brow looked towards the tower and replied, "Of course, you are a bit late to help though, I've just finished!"

Dutch smiled, descended the steps, and found his way into the field; There, the man who he estimated was in his early forties, 5'8", medium length black hair, had replaced the sweatshirt he had been wearing with a grey tee shirt. He also wore grey cargo trousers and brown working boots and was walking towards him. Dutch could immediately detect by his general demeanour and complexion that he appeared to be no stranger to the great outdoors.

Dutch opened the conversation by saying, "Hi, my name is Dennis French are you the owner of this very impressive site?"

"Yes, and flattery will get you everywhere. Ross Beare at your service, how may I help you, Buddy?"

"I happened to be passing and thought I would kill two birds with one stone, so as to speak. I have often thought of suggesting to some colleagues from the running club that I belong to, or the mountain rescue team that I have recently joined to come here for a game, and this seemed a good time to check out the facilities. At the same time, I wanted to investigate the possibility of dropping off some leaflets advertising my minibus tours. Do you think it would be worth it? I do pay a reasonable commission for any business raised."

"Do you know what, I'm surprised that any of you boys haven't thought of this angle before. During the summer I get lots of youngsters, particularly teenagers in here with their parents. What regularly happens is that families come to the area on holiday, but the kids soon get fed up with walking around looking at the lakes and countryside. Their whinging about being bored often turns into a compromise between parent and child, which leads them to here, which is about the most exciting place in these parts for the younger generation."

"Yes, but youngsters wouldn't be interested in my tours."

"You are missing the point. The parents of these kiddywinks often wait here for the duration of the game, watching their offspring shooting the hell out of each other and have a tea or coffee whilst waiting the couple of hours. Some of your leaflets left on the tables would be the only thing here to read, which may lead them to you".

"So, it could well work for us both then?"

"Sure could. Do you fancy a coffee, I'm dying for one?"

"Sounds good to me, thanks".

As they moved off, a fearsome looking Rottweiler suddenly appeared. As the dog approached Dutch, Ross noticed his concerned facial expression and quickly explained," Don't worry about the beast. His name is Blitz and he's soft, a complete disgrace to the reputation of his breed. As if to demonstrate his handlers comments the dog took a couple of sniffs of Dutch's shoes and trouser legs, then disinterested in the visitor, sloped off in the direction from which it had come.

"See what I mean? I named him Blitz after the word Blitzkrieg, a German word which you may be familiar with, it means rapid attack but that meaning is thankfully lost on that muttley like hound, but the baddies don't know that and tend not to test him."

Both men sat at the refreshment area and discussed various subjects over a hot drink, soon indulging in lengthy congenial chat.

During the conversation, Dutch, quickly considered Ross to be a very friendly and understanding person, and extremely passionate about the area in which he lived and worked. They exchanged life experiences and Dutch made mention of his lengthy Army career and made a brief reference, which he instantly regretted, that in the past he had upset an organised Eastern European criminal gang. Ross became inquisitive, but Dutch was able to divert the course of the conversation realising it was amiss of him to mention it and had mistakenly only done so because he felt extremely relaxed in Ross's company.

Ross responded that since the government's austerity policy, resulting in a lack of policing, crime in the area had increased. The comment prompted Dutch to say that since moving there someone had tried to force open the doors to the barn where he parked his bus, but they had failed as the padlocks were extremely secure. He hadn't bothered to report the unsuccessful attempt as he wouldn't expect any police reaction. What he didn't tell Ross was that he hadn't reported it, because he didn't wish to furnish his details to the police so soon after his recent experience with the Sussex force.

Following the comment Ross, who suddenly became animated about the subject said, "See, nobody trusts the police to take any interest in minor crime anymore. Like yourself, more than half the crime committed doesn't even get reported, and not much of what does gets detected. That's why additional action is required, as we all are deeply concerned."

Dutch could hear and sense his passion about the subject.

"You say that you've been in the army, so you've known discipline and the need maintain some kind of order.?"

"Yes, we all need to obey rules but there will always be some that can't or just won't, its bullies that get me though. My brothers, sisters and me had a bit of a rough time of it when we were young, which has caused me to hate those that bully. A lot of both big time and minor criminals are like that, in the way they prey on the weak and vulnerable."

"Dennis, you come across as a decent and caring human being. I would like to confide in you but if I did, I would appreciate your word not to mention what I say to anyone regarding this proposal."

"This sounds too intriguing to miss out on, so you have my word. By the way, call me by my army nickname which is Dutch. You probably get the gist, French, Dutch!"

"Okay Dutch. As I was born and bred here, I love this area and would hate it to turn into rat shit, so a small group of us 'locals', let's say look into some of the local minor crime. Nothing heavy just petty stuff like theft and public nuisance. Some would call us vigilantes, but that word is too severe, we look at ourselves as guardians of the South Lake District, and have no intentions of using any rough stuff. Believe me this whole area is one of the most beautiful and serene places on earth but if some of the visitors and inhabitants were left to their own devices the area would go downhill fast."

Ross looked at Dutch as if waiting for a response to his statement.

"That seems an excellent idea, it's good to know that there are some responsible citizens out there taking an interest in law and order in the community as the police are so thinly spread these days. What do you mean by look into?"

"Let's not beat about the bush. The town has a population of two and a half thousand, plus millions of visitors annually, yet eight years ago some clever dicks decided to close our police station and cover us from the larger stations. That decision consequently caused enough concern for some of us to form a small group to protect our patch. As a body we take note of the local issues that the police aren't dealing with and if suitable we carry out our own investigations. If we catch someone for a minor crime or manage to prevent one it is usually dealt with peacefully and amicably without informing the police. That way we can remain anonymous but on a couple of occasions when it has turned physical, or the offence is too serious, to safeguard ourselves we've had to involve the police. Luckily on the few occasions that we've had to go official, the members involved have managed to blag their way out of why they were present in the area when the crime took place. Although I've only known you for less than an hour, I am certain that with your past experience you would be of great benefit to the group. We are only a small band of men and woman and only request the assistance of the very few that we believe we can trust. We don't only get involved in local crime and general nuisance we also make ourselves available to help out in emergencies such as searching for missing persons, but in such cases, we don't disclose ourselves as an organisation."

"I am honoured that you think of me in that way. I would be interested as I am planning to spend the rest of my days here, so I should contribute to our wellbeing and in the area as a whole. Just run through how it works?"

Ross, smiling replied," Before I divulge all of our darkest secrets, I will need a firm commitment from you?"

"Okay, the deal is yes, I'm in, if I can leave my leaflets here?"

"Good man, of course you can. I would have let you leave them even if you had said no, but now you've given me more incentive to push your business. That's as long as the commission is good."

All my agents get fifteen per cent, is that okay with you?"

"That's fine. That's the business side of things out of the way. Now have you got time for me to very briefly inform you about how the group operates?"

"I was going to see some other agents, but I can do that another time, I'm too interested in this topic now."

"Pc Sleat, the longest serving local officer, who's a good cop and a nice guy, once just solely covered the town and immediate area, but is now responsible for the policing of some of the outlying towns and villages as well. He now has little time allocated for foot patrol around our town and when seen is usually driving a Land Rover from one job to another, so any policing is, as you said, spread very thinly. Details of locally committed crime and current crime trend bulletins are sent from Kendal police station to our neighbourhood watch coordinator Marylynn, who strangely enough happens to be part of our group. She in turn distributes the information to the various neighbourhood watch groups within the community, with which I happen to be involved here. We get the same info as the other groups but if we need a bit more to work on Marylynn, who has been providing the same excellent service for years is a trusted police source, so is very often able to secure extra intelligence and provide me with more details than those originally published for general public viewing.

"Pete Sleat has an inkling that somethings going on as he sees us out and about at odd times of the day and night, but he's old school and knowing that we are not up to anything illegal, asks few questions. But I suspect that he believes that whatever it may be, I am the instigator! Due to his suspicions and because the force would positively discourage the group despite our good intentions, I have had to take a back seat as far as any physical involvement in our commitments go, for a while at least; We can't afford any of our interventions to lead back to either of my sites, as that could put a complete kibosh on the network. May I ask Dutch: Have you any specific skills that would be particularly useful to us?"

Smiling he replied jovially: "I am particularly skilled in parachuting, first aid and lifesaving. I also have previous experience of shooting at people and blowing up buildings, but hopefully we won't be going quite that far! No, seriously, apart from normal soldering skills I had a second career in all things water-related, but I don't think that will particularly helpful unless we need to give anyone the waterboard treatment."

Ross laughed, "Perhaps not but you could always replace some of my dodgy taps. I'm sure that you have been involved in many clandestine operations in the past and most of what we do is at night so will be second nature to you."

"True, but I'm not sure how much time I can devote during the summer months as I hope to be extremely busy."

"Most of us are in the same position as much of the work here is seasonal, although we do have a number of members who are fully retired. As I mentioned, it generally involves unsociable hours but as we have a reasonable number to choose from something can usually be worked out between us all, after all what's a few hours lost sleep compared with rampant crime? We try to spread it across the board so that we all do an equal share. If we can't cover something, c'est la vie, we are only volunteers, but we do try one way or another to complete every job we take on. Believe me it can be very rewarding as well as exciting at times".

"If you do catch anyone committing crime you never involve the police then, because If you did surely they will realise what's going on?"

"Good question. As I mentioned we do try to avoid involving the police for that reason, and of course as a group we need to remain anonymous as none of us wish to be a witness in court. Although what we do is not illegal, if the police knew of our objectives they would certainly put pressure on us to disband the group. Because we only get involved in low level crime and most of those responsible are locals, we usually have the means to apply alternative methods to remedy the situation, obtain a favourable result for all concerned and prevent further offending. There is a real danger that if police resources are not returned as to how they once were the crime rate will soar, not only here but nationwide."

"So where do we go from here?"

"You will obviously need to meet everyone involved. Amongst our ranks are paramedics, fireman, several ex members of the armed forces like yourself, farmers, and engineers, to name but a few. There are some with no particular skills but have a pair of eyes and a wiliness to help keep this community as crime free and as law abiding as possible. The only perk for being involved is that all get the free use of my Airsoft site and facilities during the afternoons on most weekdays, excluding school holidays and corporate events."

"I obviously know what occurs at a paintball site but what actually is airsoft, as I have never heard that term before today?"

"It's very much like paintball but not so messy as the weapons fire small plastic balls instead of paint. The only disadvantage is that some unscrupulous players can deny being hit, as unlike paint the ammunition doesn't leave any marks on clothing. The airsoft site does not only cater for target and tactical shooting there is also an assortment of other activities that may well appeal to an active man such as yourself. These include a Segway experience, axe throwing, archery, a rally dirt track for our 4X4s, and just for you, an assault course which includes a cold-water plunge pool. That's it in a nutshell! Well, we had both better get back to work. I'll let you know the next time when you can come along and meet some of the crew. We get together every first Monday of the month but if anything crops up in between times that the police are not actively dealing with but needs some attention we will seek volunteers. Just in case that happens, all text communications amongst the group are worded in a way that the messages could relate to the normal activities that go on here. Any questions?"

"No, you've been very clear, and I will soon get to know the ropes. Just one thing, your businesses seems to be spread over a vast area. How many acres do you have altogether?"

"Seventy-six acres, mostly woodland which contains plenty of wildlife including pheasants and rabbits, so if you own a shotgun you are most welcome to use it from time to time. Any game that we get is sold to the pubs or restaurants and the money goes towards group funds for any extra equipment that we may need."

"Thanks, but no thanks, game shooting is not my bag."

"I should have known that as a previous soldier, shooting humans would be more up your street."

Both men laughed, but as soon as the words had left Ross's lips, Dutch knew that even if he was interested in possessing a shotgun there was no way that he could chance applying for a shotgun certificate, as to prove his competence to own the weapon would entail the police searching the police national computer, and although he had no previous criminal convictions recorded, he did not know if there was any intelligence recorded regarding his previous suspected activities. If this were to be revealed, not only would such an application fail but would also alert the local constabulary to his darker past.

Having said their farewells and swapped telephone numbers, before departing Dutch distributed some of his leaflets on the wooden dining tables. As arranged, he would await a message from Ross as to when they would next meet.

During the following day, when the opportunity arose between tour bookings, Dutch took the opportunity to visit further agents and whist doing so he received a call from the Mayor of the town who explained that he had just reserved some rooms at a local hotel for what he described as special visitors. The visitors would require a reliable 'ad hoc' form of transport during their week-long visit and the hotel concerned had recommended him. Would he be interested in committing to the work?

It was a 'no brainer' for Dutch as not only would it be a good earner to transport special guests for a local dignitary, he also considered that if it went well, it would be a feather in his cap, perhaps leading to further similar work from the reputable source. Having accepted the proposed terms and answered a few questions regarding the validity of his vehicle documentation, the Mayor asked him if he had heard of The Windermere Children?

Such a question surprised Dutch, but after brief hesitation, he asked if he was referring to the group of young orphaned Jewish refugees who survived the Holocaust, and, following the war were brought to nearby Troutbeck Bridge. When the Mayor confirmed his statement, Dutch was pleased that he was able to demonstrate that, as a newbie to the area, he had gained such useful knowledge while studying the local history for possible use in his tours.

His reply pleased the Mayor immensely, who then told Dutch that the passengers were the descendants of some of those children, who wished to see the surroundings to where their late family members had been evacuated.

He confirmed that Dutch had the job and he would be sent an email confirming the details of the appointment.

At the completion of the call Dutch ran over in his head as to what he could remember from his research.

In 1945 about 300 traumatised Jewish children, girls and boys who had survived the Nazi death camps, were evacuated to the shores of lake Windermere to help them rehabilitate and rebuild their lives. With no surviving parents they were billeted on a disused factory site on the Calgarth Estate and cared for by a team of child psychologists, counsellors, and teachers. After a year many were found new homes and remained in the U.K for the rest of their lives. Some became very successful in business and received national recognition for their services, others gained the status of world class athletes. Most had now passed away, but a small number still survive.

The village of Troutbeck Bridge was only three miles from Ambleside, but as the Mayor had confirmed that as he would be the only transport for the group, and as their itinerary included visiting much of the district and surrounding towns he would be kept busy for the week and well rewarded for his efforts. This appeared to be a good omen for the season's business prospects.

To communicate even further knowledge to his future passengers he again watched the BBC drama film based on the event and attended the library to read some more local literature on the subject.

CHAPTER 3

Dirty Ol' Man *(1973)*

Artists: Three Degrees
Writers: K. Gamble, L. Huff

Only a few days after his initial meeting with Ross, Dutch received a phone call which indicated that Ross was the caller.

"Hi Ross, how are you doing?"

"Good thanks Dutch. Somethings come up; I know this is a bit off the cuff, but I think it's a great opportunity for you to see what we are all about."

"Carry on, I'm all ears."

"How are you at getting up early, say 4am tomorrow morning? No pressure as I can always find someone else if not convenient?"

"I've always been an early riser and was once on call out at all ungodly hours, so no probs."

"Are you able to meet me at the barn, say at six this evening?"

"Yep that should be fine, my last tour should be over by five today."

"Okay, see you there."

Once the call concluded Dutch was intrigued as to what he may have volunteered for and thought of the old army maxim, never volunteer for anything, but he understood why Ross was reluctant to go into too much detail on the phone.

Dutch was ten minutes early for his meeting and as soon as he entered the barn he was confronted with Ross and another man talking together outside a two-storey wooden, camouflaged construction on one side of the vast interior. He immediately noticed that the remainder of the space was taken up by the equipment and rooms required by the removal and mobile fish and chip companies, whose vehicles were parked outside.

Ross immediately introduced him to the short portly man as Tim, who Dutch estimated as about forty years of age.

Following introductions, Ross suggested that before getting to the point of the meeting that he gave Dutch a tour of the armoury. Dutch followed both men and before entering the ground floor of the wooden structure he noticed a large cage containing numerous bags of camouflaged tunics. Once inside the room he was surprised as to the mass of weapons on display, mostly very realistic assault rifles and pistols together with longbows and arrows. There were also numerous cardboard boxes, marked paintballs, airsoft pellets, grenades, flares, and smoke grenades. On one side of the room was a large work bench containing numerous tools and weapons in various stages of repair. Dutch also recognised what he knew to be an arrow straightening device. Ross invited Dutch to examine one of the airsoft rifles and he was impressed as to how realistic it was to the genuine Heckler and Koch G36 military assault rifle, of which he had previous knowledge. All three men agreed that if not on site and someone pointed it at them they would not be sure if it were the genuine article or not.

At the conclusion of the tour Ross ushered the two newly acquainted men up the wooden staircase into his office.

The room, which contained chairs and two desks, had a large window which overlooked the whole interior of the barn. The three remaining walls were littered with various papers, photographs, and whiteboards.

Once seated around what was obviously Ross's personal desk that displayed photos of his family, Ross placed an architectural street plan in the centre of the desk.

Dutch immediately recognised the names of the streets depicted on the map as those of Ambleside. He also noted that there were three red spots on what appeared to be the rear gardens of some of the dwellings.

Ross then explained, "This is a map that Marylynn has expertly produced to show exactly the problem that we need to tackle. Over the last two weeks, coinciding with the dry warmer weather the annual phantom knicker nicker has once again raised his ugly head. He was nearly caught last year when someone saw him making off, and by the description we had a good idea of his identity, but the series of thefts stopped, and we presumed it was because of his close shave in nearly getting caught. It appears that this new season with washing being left out overnight has tempted him back into his old ways. There have only been three such thefts from washing lines reported so far, but it may progress like last year, when it only stopped because he was disturbed. The only response so far from the police is to advise householders not to leave their washing to dry on the line overnight, especially women's underwear. As a group we don't feel that some sexual deviant should dictate when and what we can leave in or gardens, either day or night. Tim, as you have already done some preparation earlier today, do you want to carry on?"

"Cheers Ross. As I live in that area, I have a particular interest. The description of the pervert seen last summer was of a very tall stocky man wearing a cap. This description only really fitted one person in the immediate area and it just so happens that he is known to get up early in the morning, take his dog for a short walk before he drives his burger van down to his pitch in the lay by on the by-pass. What I plan to do is get my missus to put some of her smalls on the line tonight together with some very erotic kit that I persuaded her to purchase from the Ann Summers catalogue, then having baited the hook you and me Dutch, sit up and wait in my garden shed. We know that he was disturbed between five and five thirty. My personal theory is after getting up he walks his dog around the nearby streets looking in the back gardens for the undies that turn him on. As there was no dog seen when he was nearly caught, I am thinking after sussing out the job he takes the dog home and then returns for his ill-gotten gains before leaving for work."

Ross then said to Dutch, "One of the reasons that I chose you for this particular job is that during our first conversation you mentioned that you were a keen runner so if this bloke turns up and makes a run for it, it will be down to you to catch him because you only have to take one look at Tim to see he's built for comfort not speed. What do you think Dutch, are you okay with this?"

Tim smiling interjected "Cheeky bugger!"

Dutch still chuckling, "It sounds good to me, but Tim what do you think of the chances of him taking the bait on the very first morning of doing this sortie?"

Good as long as it's not raining. If it is, I will postpone it as I doubt if he will want to get wet and carry sodden material about. I will also have a hunt around this evening to ensure that none of the neighbours have any panties or bras on their lines as we don't want any competition do we."

"If it is this bloke, I'm not sure if I would want one of his burgers, as all kinds of weird images come to mind. Where and when do we meet then, Tim?"

Tim then placed a finger on one of the numbered houses on the map.

"That's my place, if you go around the back the number is on the unlocked wooden gate. If you get there about four thirty, I will be in the shed. Make sure that you bring your mobile as one of us may need to take photos."

Dutch took note of Tim's address and shortly before they parted company Ross suggested that both men had an early night.

Even though Dutch was well conversant with early morning rising he did not feel joy at the sounding of his Amazon Alexa alarm at 3.45 am. The disturbance caused Melanie to stir but she did not fully awake as over the years she had got used to Dutch's sometimes unannounced nocturnal habits. She would always investigate his reason for the annoyance later in the day.

He was grateful that it was a warm dry morning as he parked and locked his mountain cycle in Tim's front garden before walking to the rear of the terraced block.

After entering the garden through the rear wooden gate marked twelve, Dutch tentatively opened the shed door where inside in the semi darkness, Tim was sitting on a padded garden chair drinking from a cup and holding a flask. Tim indicated for Dutch to sit away from the window in the vacant chair next to him and confirm that his mobile was on silent mode. Without speaking Tim gestured that Dutch joined in him in a hot drink. As they both sat sipping the coffee all conversation between them was whispered and kept to a minimum. It was then that Dutch learnt that Tim was a former merchant seaman and now a water bailiff.

After what seemed longer than the thirty-five-minute wait both men froze as they heard the sound of the metal latch of the garden gate opening. Both men slowly stood and quietly sidled towards the side of the window, at the same time Tim indicated by hand gestures for Dutch to ready his telephone to take photographs. As they both peered through the window from the darkness at the rear of the shed they saw a tall, well-built man wearing a baseball cap select an item from the well-stocked washing line and stuff it in a pocket. The intruder was about to remove a further item when Dutch proceeded to take several photographs of the occurring theft. It was then that Tim opened the shed door and hurried outside saying, "Okay that's it you've been nabbed."

The thief momentarily stood still with a look of panic on his face. Sensing that the intruder was going to make a bolt for the only exit, Dutch ran to the gate and firmly planted himself in front of it. He took up the position not a moment too soon as the offender with his superior height and strength easily pushed away Tim's attempt to halt him. As he reached the gate he was confronted with the battle-hardened face and more formidable figure of Dutch, who said in a very determined tone, "You are not leaving here until you agree to speak to us. If you kick up I will have no choice but to take you to the ground which will wake everyone in the terrace, and they will soon catch on as to what you were up to. The other alternative is that we go outside into a quiet part of the street and discuss this sensibly, which depending on your cooperation may or may not involve the police?"

The man who was standing in a threatening stance only inches away from Dutch, listened intently and looking straight at him replied, "Alright let's do that, just let me out of here before someone else sees me."

As they left the garden Dutch noticed a woman who he presumed was Tim's wife had been disturbed and was peering out of a bedroom window.

Tim led them into convenience of a nearby bus shelter during in which time Dutch kept a close eye on the seemingly nervous individual.

Tim did the majority of the talking and ascertained the man's name was Trevor Russell who confirmed he was the fast-food vendor suspected of the thefts. After being asked to turn out his pockets he produced a red lace bra, which he readily admitted taking from Tim's line, at the same time continually looking about him and pleading with his captors not to involve the police.

When asked why he stole the underwear and what he did with his ill-gotten gains, Russell's explanation was that since his wife had been diagnosed with a long-term illness, coupled with problems surrounding his failing business he had become increasingly depressed. He admitted he knew that what he was doing was wrong, and that it appeared depraved, but the excitement of stealing the erotic garments helped release his anxiety. He explained that the euphoria lasted only momentarily and when he reached his burger van he immediately disposed of them in a roadside bin next to his pitch.

Neither Tim or Dutch truly believed his explanation and told him so but did not labour the point. Regardless of what perverted actions he did with the items, they really did not wish to know, and it was unlikely that through embarrassment he was ever likely to admit his true use for them.

Russell was told that even if they could recover any of the items the losers would certainly not want them returned.

At first he denied any other similar offences in the area, either shortly before or during the previous year. He was subsequently told that his denials would require further police investigation as they would need to establish if there was another similar thief operating in the same location. This statement caused Russell to admit to all nine offences that had been previously been reported to the police.

The admission was a relief to both captors who explained that they could now deal with the matter without police involvement if he were to pay all nine victims' full compensation for the items that he had stolen and apparently disposed of.

Russell readily agreed to do so and was reminded by Dutch that if he failed to pay there were photographs of him in the commission of the crime. Dutch then showed the culprit the photos that he had taken. Russell was also reminded that they knew where he lived and worked, and life could be made both difficult and embarrassing for him should he fail to pay the compensation, or if he continued committing any future crime whatsoever. There would be no second chances.

Tim informed Russell that he was in a position to find out the exact value of all the stolen goods and he would carry out the further necessary discreet communications with him at his workplace. Although his costs would not be excessive he was left in no doubt that it was not only the monetary loss to the injured parties, but also the distress it caused to the women involved, especially as they did not understand his motives, and they were very upset that he had trespassed on their property whilst they were asleep.

A very relieved and appreciative Russell then left, not appreciating that the only reason that the police had not been alerted was because the group could not afford to cause any further suspicion within police ranks regarding their clandestine activities.

Following Russell's departure Tim and Dutch discussed their suspicions as to what he did in fact do with the underwear and were jovially inquisitive as to if he was in fact wearing any of the previous stolen garments whilst they were speaking to him.

Tim informed Dutch that he would get Ross to request Marylynn to ascertain the details of the thefts, and value of all the stolen items from police crime reports, and then he would subsequently reimburse the victims following receipt of payment from Russell. Both men then congratulated each other on a rewarding result, mentioning that they would possibly next meet at the group meeting the following Monday.

Whilst eating his breakfast, Melanie appeared weary eyed from the bedroom immediately asking Dutch as to the reason for his early morning departure.

He tentatively explained how he had joined the ranks of the defenders and the details of the morning's events.

Melanie was far from overjoyed at this revelation as she could imagine as to how his new venture could turn into even further dramas that had followed him all of his life. But, from personal experience, she could appreciate the benefit of such an organisation, and knew only too well that not all victims of crime would, for various reasons, report certain matters to the police.

Melanie was devoted to her husband but could not understand how a man who apparently was now passionately seeking peace in his life would continue to pursue adventure with all the risks involved and commented:

"On the face of it, in an ideal world, this syndicate is a good idea but it could be perceived by most as a bunch of vigilantes who sort out problems by using violence like in the movies. Do you really know what you are getting yourself into?"

"I know that word Vigilante conjures up adventures by Charles Bronson and Clint Eastwood, but I'm assured that they are not like that and seek the most peaceful and amicable way to deal with matters. If it is anything else but that, I will pull out."

"It's up to you Dennis, but be careful."

Since their move he had taken up fell running and joined the mountain rescue team, both of which could provide their own form of danger. Now he had added additional risks by joining what she thought of as a secret crime busting squad. As much as she wished he did not possess such an adventurous nature, she knew that it was in his psyche and that would not change. If she were able to stop him participating in his current activities she knew it would only be a matter of time until he would drift into other equally hazardous situations. When Dutch was a younger man her mother, Molly, would on occasions affectionally refer to him as Peter Pan, comparing him to the fictitious boy who wouldn't grow up, penned in the book of that name by J.M. Barrie. Despite his age her husband was still a visionary, a compulsive runner, regularly listening to pop music from a bygone era and still playing boyish pranks associated with a much younger man. She did not wish to be responsible in curtailing his enthusiasm for life, which her mother had recognised all those years ago.

Whilst Melanie had these thoughts she was unaware of the far more murderous threat which continued to follow them, of which her husband had failed to inform her.

CHAPTER 4

Getting Started *(2019)*

Artist: Aloe Blacc
Writer: Kyle Williams

The planning and organisation leading to the apprehension of Russell had impressed Dutch. Not only had he enjoyed the excitement of the catch, but also felt that he was contributing to the good of the community, because a series of crimes may have continued and never been detected if the group had not intervened.

His keenness to be further involved was soon rewarded when he received a call from Ross congratulating him with his contribution earlier in the day and asking him if he would wish to join some of the other members of the group at the following Monday evenings' monthly meeting. Ross informed him that these meetings took place at the airsoft centre, and for their privacy the main entrance barrier would be locked, therefore he would need to access the site from a one-mile woodland track leading from the remote Parish Lane. To deter unwanted visitors to the site, there were no signs indicating the facility, so Ross gave him explicit directions and suggested that he arrive half an hour early so he could give him a brief tour of the site. Dutch was pleased with the invitation as he had been extremely impressed with what he had experienced so far and was looking forward to participating in all of the activities on offer.

It had been raining for most of the Monday prior to the meeting, but as Dutch drove along the narrow Parish Lane searching for the woodland track that Ross had described, the rain stopped and the grey clouds cleared giving way to a pleasant evening. Having located the entrance to the site he drove along the track and found the mud surface covered by years of fallen pine needles flat and pleasant to drive on. He took the opportunity to open his window and breathe in the scent emitted from the tall straight, wet pines.

Having travelled deep into the forest Dutch became aware of how difficult it would be to locate the remote site from the public road without specific directions. His journey concluded at a large gravel covered clearing where he parked close to the two cars present. As he alighted and walked towards the entrance which was almost identical to that of the paintball site, and also controlled by a metal security arm, with a further machine gun post, and a single large grey missile on the verge close by. Dutch was intrigued as to where on earth Ross had obtained such large and heavy projectiles. On entering the compound comprised of a mass of low wooden log buildings, he saw Ross standing next to another man who also was standing and resting his elbows on a tall wooden bench, aiming, and firing what Dutch now knew to be a G36 airsoft rifle. He was aiming at a narrow set of targets of various sizes situated between an avenue of pines, all of which were encompassed by fine gauge safety netting. Both men, who had their backs to him, and wearing ear defenders, were unaware of his approach. As soon as the salvo was over, Dutch made his presence known, prompting Ross to turn around and address both men.

"Dutch, this is Chip a long-standing member of our exclusive club, he's formerly royal navy engineer, now a forestry worker but we don't hold that against him! Dutch is our newest member who I'm going to show around the site prior to tonight's meeting."

Chip jovially replied, "This takes me back to my first visit here, Ross was very nice and polite to me then, but don't worry it soon goes downhill."

Ross immediately responded with an indecent hand gesture followed by Chip remarking: "What do you do with yourself Dutch, when you are not visiting this reprobate?"

"Self-employed minibus tour operator now but spent most of my life in the Army."

"Really, take this then and show us how it's done."

Chip checked that the safety catch was engaged and tossed the weapon that he was holding to Dutch.

After closely inspecting the rifle Dutch leant on the firing table, took careful aim and after verbally indicating that he was aiming at the furthest target, pulled the trigger.

Ross, who was viewing the target through a set of binoculars retrieved from a nearby peg, commented: "Not bad for first shot Dutch, just off centre."

"Good I'm pleased with that. I was once a qualified sniper, but I wasn't going to mention that before in case it went badly wrong."

"Ross was telling me about the good result that you had catching Trevor Russell. I always thought he was an odd ball."

"He's definitely got issues, that's for sure."

Ross interrupted, "Talking about issues tell Dutch about your infamous capture Chip."

"It's not a tale for the faint-hearted Dutch and I will have to tell the whole story for it to make any sense."

Ross then said, "Hurry it up then Chip, the meeting starts in twenty-five minutes. Dutch is a man of the world."

"Okay, a local farmer Dan Walker had a nasty accident when his tractor overturned into a ditch. Whilst he was in hospital, his wife Fay, with a little help from others carried on running the farm.

"During Dan's hospitalisation Fay became increasingly concerned about objects being moved about the fields at night. As on each occasion nothing had been damaged or stolen, she believed that the trespassers may be satanic worshippers and mentioned the fact to her local neighbourhood watch member, the information was then relayed to Marylynn.

"When Ross mentioned it, I and one other foolhardy person stepped forward not knowing what horrors awaited."

Dutch started chuckling saying: "This is some build up; it better be good!"

"I assure you it isn't good."

Ross interjected, "For fuck sake Chip, we don't need chapter and verse."

Chip depicting a fanning motion with his hands: "Calm down, I have to set the scene for maximum impact."

Chip then continued talking and it became obvious that he was winding Ross up by slowly relaying every little detail.

"So, me and the other guy staked out the field concerned which was inhabited by some rare breed cattle. Due to Fay's suspicions we were half expecting a group of hooded habit wearing loonies to turn up, so we were surprised when a lone male entered the field. The first thing he did was to grab hold of one the smaller empty oil drums from a corner of the field and roll it up behind one of the cows. We were surprised that despite his presence none of the herd appeared unsettled regarding his movements. The next thing that happened left me dumbstruck. This individual steadied the drum in the mud, stood on it, undid his trousers and although it was dark, but unfortunately not dark enough as I could still make out that he was actually shagging the cow, which still hadn't moved an inch.

"We couldn't bear to watch the depravity for a second more and jumped out of hiding place. On seeing us the dirty bastard jumped off the drum and must have forgotten that his trousers were down around his ankles because as he tried to run from us, slid on a cowpat, fell arse overhead and got covered in cow shit. Can you just imagine the scene as we stood over this bloke who was covered in fresh wet crap, fully exposed from the waist down and stinking like a sewer. He was a small scrawny individual who continued to lay there pleading with us not to hit him, but there was no chance of us touching him in any way whatsoever. To be honest, after witnessing that, we just wanted to get out of there as soon as possible. We established his name and the fact that he was a relief morning dairyman at the farm in the absence of Dan. It then became obvious to me and my partner as to why the cow was so passive, as the pervert milked the entire herd every day. There was no way we were going to go official on this. For one, as always we needed to keep our anonymity, and secondly no police officer was going to thank us for apprehending a weirdo covered from head to foot in cow muck.

"After establishing where he was staying and telling him that he had lost his job and never to enter the farm grounds again, I took some photos on my mobile of him standing next to his bovine lover. Then he was strongly advised that if he were found doing anything similar again, the photos would be made public. I swear if I showed you those photo's you would agree that the cow had a smile on her face."

Dutch exclaimed, "No, no, far too much information, that story will be etched in my memory forever! Please tell me you have just made that up?"

"I'm afraid it's perfectly true. Believe me the situation got even worse. Can you imagine, I had to knock Fay up, who is a very prim and proper lady and tell her not only had she lost her dairyman but also what we had seen him do. I later found out that the offence of bestiality can result in two years jail, so he can think himself lucky, if it had gone to court the publicity would have been more than a little embarrassing."

Dutch then burst out laughing evoking Ross to say, "You should have heard some of the comments aimed at both of them when I mentioned it at the next meeting. I can remember one wit asking Chip if he thought the cow had experienced the earth mooooove."

What's tickling you Dutch?"

"I was just wondering if when that filthy fucker milked the cows in the morning he considered that as foreplay and then returned to finish the dirty deed later. If you think about it he may have the right idea as he didn't have to buy the cow flowers or take it to dinner before having sex."

All three playfully agreed it was definitely the cheaper option to normal dating but didn't relish the thought of indulging in the activity any time soon.

Ross interjected: "I'm sure that you would both like to continue shooting but Dutch and I need to get this tour done before the meeting starts."

Both men then left Chip to continue his practice as they ambled round the numerous buildings, which similar to the paintball site, housed a check in desk, ammunition shop, large competition blackboard and a refreshment hut. The majority of the other wooden huts contained tables and chairs which Ross explained were bays where players would sit, load, or clean their weapons.

After leaving the buildings they followed through a passageway enclosed in safety netting and entered the war games site. This was a large area of woodland, and among the many trees there were further numerous white, crudely built wooden hides. As the site needed little explanation Ross continued to walk through the woods until they emerged from the canopy onto a narrow muddy track where at intervals there were steep hillocks, deep troughs, and severe bends. Dutch correctly guessed by the numerous tyre impressions, that it was the 4X4 driving experience course which took his mind back to his army days when driving various types of combat vehicles on similar terrain. He made Ross aware that he was keen to drive the course at the earliest opportunity. Owing to the imminent meeting the pair were forced to hurry about the remaining activity sites which encircled a large well-manicured grass field. At various intervals there were further numerous log-built huts, identical to the many others that he had seen previously. The covered buildings gave access to grassed archery target ranges and an axe throwing target area. On and around the green expanse many obstacles associated with an assault course were present. In the centre of the field was cargo netting, large truck tyres, high wooden obstacles, and a stack of hay bales. At the side of the obstacles, within a clump of small trees a small man-made pool could be seen.

On checking their watches, and both confirming it was 7.25, they hurriedly returned to the activity centre. As they reached the clearing Dutch saw that there were now at least an additional eight cars parked close to his own transport. On entering the complex, he estimated that there were approximately eight men and two women standing at the refreshment bar helping themselves to tea from a large chrome urn. On seeing Dutch, Tim broke away from the group and spoke with him whilst Ross joined the throng, and, after much banter with the group he returned to Dutch with a hot cup of tea.

After calling for order and obtaining silence from the jovial and energetic group, Ross then introduced Dutch. He informed them of Tim and Dutch's recent exploit with the underwear thief, which resulted in a spontaneous round of applause joined by comments such as knicker less Nickleby, Undie-niable success, basking in the knickerbocker glory. All the comments and leg pulling reminded Dutch of many similar piss-taking situations whilst in the mob.

The meeting chaired by Ross, then took on a more formal note with apologies for absence, the reviewing of the most recent crime from the neighbourhood watch bulletin, and any further issues that had come to the attention of the group members themselves, or from local newspaper reports. As there was little in the way of crime matters that the group could involve themselves in there was a general discussion amongst all present as to which current problems they should prioritise. The general consensus of opinion was to target occurring fly tipping episodes, and a prolific graffiti artist operating in and around the town centre. One of the two ladies present announced that she had suspicion as to the ownership of the most prevalent graffiti tag being used and volunteered to investigate further. Another attendee quickly came forward to assist her.

It was Ross's usual practice at each meeting to provide his audience with an interesting crime related anecdote, and this occasion was no exception. His theme was that all reported crime may not be as it seems. He told of how it had come to his notice that a man had recently reported parking his car outside a local fish and chip shop, and whilst inside the shop it had been stolen. Unfortunately for the apparent loser of the vehicle, who did not live in the immediate area, made the report to a police officer who regularly used the shop in question. When giving his statement the apparently aggrieved party told the officer that his car had been stolen on a Monday evening whilst he was inside the shop for ten minutes waiting to purchase his supper. Due to his suspicions the constable asked the informant to confirm the day that the offence took place, and he was again told it happened on the Monday. The officer did not immediately reveal that he knew that the shop in question was never open for business on that day of the week and obtained the full details of the alleged stolen vehicle. The officer then spent the next day visiting the scrap metal and vehicle salvage yards over a widespread area, eventually discovering the vehicle in question, minus its number plates ready for the crusher. The car owner was subsequently arrested and pleaded guilty at court for the attempted deception of his insurance company and wasting police time, which cost him a huge fine, far more than what it would have cost him to put the MOT failure back on the road. The group agreed that this was yet another example of how vital it was that police officers should again be permanently based within the community.

After Ross confirmed the date of the next meeting the group dispersed by either leaving the venue or obtaining further tea and sitting chatting on the benches. Dutch took the opportunity to make himself known to most of those remaining but hurried his introductions as he had been away from home since early morning.

Melanie had not mentioned anything to him, but he became to realise that with his two occupations and numerous hobbies, together with the introduction of this new venture he was spending less and less time in her company. He loved his wife dearly and as much as he wished to be in her company he had always been an adventurous and energetic person who needed to be constantly busy, and with all the interesting activities at hand he was finding constant difficulty in juggling both his personal and married life. Melanie had always been understanding of his particular interests, but in order to give her the attention that she deserved, he would need to get away from all of the distractions and take her away on a break, by way of an apology for his regular absenteeism.

The following evening, having recognised his failings towards Melanie, he purchased take away meals for them both and his in-laws. Following a pleasant dinner, he spoke to his wife alone about his guilty feelings. Much to his surprise, Melanie was amused at his concern, explaining that he had never been any different and that she had accepted that was him a long time ago, and it would be inconceivable for her to expect that he could suddenly change. She didn't think any the less of him for spending so much time engaged at work or with his interests, as long as he was happy and returned home safe and well. When Dutch suggested that they went on a short break he was surprised that rather than choose a week abroad, Melanie gave her preference to a few days holidaying in Liverpool, as she didn't wish to travel too far away from her ageing parents. Sensing his surprise at her choice of venue, she explained that it was a city that she had never visited and wished to see the sights, shop at the renowned Liverpool One shopping precinct, and also visit her cousin Tracy and her family. Although amazed, Dutch was pleased at her decision as when in his early twenties he had only spent a limited time in the city during a short stag party weekend with fellow soldiers. The only drawback was his regret that it was during that weekend, he, for the one and only time during their long marriage, had been unfaithful to Melanie and slept with someone he had just met, Kerry. Melanie was completely unaware of his transgression, but the episode had recently come back to haunt him as, by chance after twenty-one years, he and Kerry met for the first time since their one night together. From their conversation then, Dutch came to the realisation that he was possibly the father of her son, Andrew. Both were in agreement that to reveal such a revelation would disrupt both of their happy family lives, so they would continue to keep their secret from both parties.

Whilst pondering on his misdemeanour he had no idea that he had not heard the last of the subject.

Dutch was true to his word: In less than a week he had booked their accommodation, and Melanie had ensured that her parents, and their ever-faithful dog Jodie, had all that they needed whilst they were away in Liverpool.

Their 95-mile journey terminated at a large three-story Victorian house situated on the top of a steep residential road in New Brighton on the Wirral Peninsula. Their immaculately presented third floor rented apartment facilitated stunning panoramic views over both the majestic, yet murky waters of the renowned river Mersey and the buildings of the city of Liverpool beyond.

No sooner had they unpacked when Melanie's cousin Tracy and her daughter Beth arrived to take them for a tour of the peninsular.

Among the sites visited included the impressive twelfth century Birkenhead priory and the scenic village of Parkgate, from where the coast of Wales was clearly visible across the river Dee. The very pleasant day concluded with the consumption of a fine meal at an Italian restaurant where they met with Tracy's husband Stu, and her mother Mavis. Dutch was pleased to see Melanie so much more relaxed in the company of the very pleasant, but few surviving members of her family, which made him realise that he should try to afford her more of his time in the future for similar trips.

The following day Melanie, like Dutch many years before, fulfilled her wish to travel on a ferry across the Mersey. It was a journey that she enjoyed immensely, taking countless photographs of the sights of the city's waterfront and the all-important selfie with the larger than life statue of the Beatles situated at Pier Head and close to the majestic buildings known as The Three Graces. The remaining days of the vacation were taken up by Melanie fully immersing herself in exploring the variety of shops that were not generally available to her, and visiting the works of celebrated street artists such as Paul Curtis, followed by a trip to the 900 listed village buildings at Port Sunlight. Dutch did indulge a little time for himself by taking in a football match at Prenton Park the home of Tranmere Rovers in company with Stu, a huge Rovers fan. On the final day, for his finale Dutch surprised his wife by taking her to the Cheshire Oaks designer outlet at Ellesmere Port where she browsed the units for hours.

During those few days away together, which both agreed was a wonderful experience, Dutch detected a change in his wife. Not only was she fully relaxed and happy in the company of her family but she had regained the self confidence that she had possessed in abundance before the ordeals of her two miscarriages, the brutal rape, and the stress that Dutch had caused by his impulsive actions in search of retribution.

CHAPTER 5

Bad Boys *(1987)*

Artists: Inner Circle
Writer: Ian Lewis

Soon after returning home Dutch honoured his agreement with the Mayor by commencing his week-long commitment in transporting the descendants of the Windermere children.

As he had made a point of studying the history of the young refugees, Dutch was able to give an informative tour of the area of what was once the Calgarth Estate constructed for former wartime aircraft factory workers which had proved to be suitable accommodation for the displaced children. Much of the week was taken up by transporting the group on his usual Lakeland tours interspersed with trips into some of the further afield villages and towns. It was during the evening following one such tour that Dutch received a call from Ross.

Following the usual pleasantries Ross gave the reason for his call.

"I apologise for asking you this so soon after your last job, but I am desperate for a suitable person to accompany another member of the group in an effort to stop reoccurring thefts from a supermarket in the town. I have a few volunteers for an early morning this week, but we may well need a bit of muscle for this one as we haven't a clue who we are dealing with. Any possibility that you could be available. It's happening so regularly that there is a good chance of a catch, so thought that you may be interested?"

Dutch's first thoughts were to make an excuse of a work commitment, or a similar reason as he was conscious that this would be yet another distraction from his family life which he had intended to adjust. On the other hand, he didn't want to let Ross or the team down and if the commitment proved as exciting and rewarding as catching of the pantie thief the temptation was too great for him to resist. If he turned the opportunity down he knew that he would instantly regret the decision. Ross had him hooked, he was the dealer and Dutch was the adrenalin junkie.

"Okay count me in, as long as its early morning and won't interfere with my work schedule."

"Brilliant. It's a situation that occurs very early so you will probably even have the chance of going back to bed before work. You will be with a chap named Howard who knows all about the problem, so the best thing I can do is give you his number and you can work it out between you."

Having obtained the number, without delay Dutch made the call and arranged to meet Howard later that evening at the rear of the local Sugdens supermarket.

On arrival he met with Howard and the shop manager who introduced himself as Tony. Dutch vaguely knew Tony, as Melanie and he regularly shopped in the store, and he was usually present on the shop floor at most times of the day. Tony was of Asian origin, tall, slim, and very well presented.

He spoke in a soft articulate tone as he pointed to a brick-built storeroom attached to the rear of the shop premises in the loading bay area. Tony explained that a consignment of bread and cakes were delivered to the storeroom each morning by a vast nationally known company between the hours of 3.30 am and 4 am, and, sometime between then and the shop staff arriving at 7.30, products were being stolen from the storeroom. He added that the persons responsible were being particularly devious as they were only taking small amounts at a time, approximately every other day and he felt that they were doing this in the hope that the small loss from the large order would go unnoticed. Although the items stolen didn't appear to be of great value, a recent stocktake revealed that the thefts had been continuing over a number of weeks.

Dutch was about to ask why the storeroom was not locked following the delivery, when Tony continued to explain that they had tried all methods of leaving a key in a hidden place or leaving a key with the driver, or in the delivery vehicles, but because the company was so vast it was not always the same driver or vehicle, and messages about the location of the key were not passed on. The confusion regarding the key had meant that on occasions the delivery had not been left at all, or had been left out in all weathers, or at the mercy of foxes. As Tony worked a fourteen-hour day he thought it unfair that he should have to get up so early in the morning to accept the delivery, and none of his staff were willing to do so despite him offering them a monetary incentive. He had reported the matter to the police and they suggested that he should get the storeroom alarmed, or a combination key safe. But, neither would solve the problem as, if an alarm sounded, it would require Tony to leave his flat above the shop and possibly have to confront the thief alone, as the chances of any police officers being anywhere nearby were slim. Also, he had no confidence in a combination number being passed on by the numerous delivery drivers.

It was agreed between the three that as there had not been a theft that morning, then according to the pattern there was a good chance of one happening in only a few hours from then. With this in mind Howard and Dutch took a brief look inside the storeroom noting that the only contents were shopping trollies and baskets, together with stacks of plastic grocery trays and numerous empty cardboard boxes. After a brief consultation, the three men piled up both the boxes and trays into a wall type structure at the rear of the storeroom. Having made their hide both men said their farewells to Tony and went straight to their respective homes for an early night. Before going to bed Dutch thought that for once it was prudent for him to tell Melanie why he was planning to get up so early. He had expected a frustrated response, but to his surprise as she enjoyed shopping at the supermarket and had got to know Tony quite well, Melanie was agreeable with him assisting the likeable manager in any way he could.

Dutch had never been a man who needed a lot of sleep and felt surprisingly bright when he met Howard in the loading bay at 3am. Both men then entered the storeroom, briefly switching on the internal light to ensure everything was how they had left it.

Once plunged into complete darkness, they concealed themselves behind the barrier of crates and boxes. During their wait they leant against the shopping trollies, occasionally conversing in whispers.

Dutch noted that it was about 3.30 am when the eerie silence was broken by the sound of the loud engine of a large lorry approaching the loading bay. As the lorry came to a halt the hissing of the air brakes reverberated around the walls of the loading bay. The driver was obviously paying little heed to the sleeping occupants in the flats above as the sound of doors being slammed, followed by the sound of the wheels of a trolly on the hard surface was clearly audible. As the trolley reached the closed door of the storeroom, the noise of falling objects was heard by both men inside, this was swiftly followed by a tirade of expletives, containing almost every swear word known to man.

As the driver continued to rant and curse at his misfortune, both Howard and Dutch had to tightly press their hands over their mouths to prevent them laughing out loud. After the driver had reloaded the trolley, the storeroom door was robustly pushed open causing the entire area to be illuminated by the headlights of the parked lorry, leaving the two observers feeling vulnerable behind their makeshift hide. Both Howard and Dutch could now see that each of them were struggling to restrain their amusement, made more difficult when the driver started to forcibly slide the bins through the door, and with each one dispatched, he swore at it as if it was a disobedient pet. Both men with tears running down their cheeks started to chortle, which fortunately was masked by the disparaging words of the angry driver and his throbbing diesel engine.

Once the door was closed and they had heard the lorry drive off, both men burst out into loud uninhibited laughter. When composed Dutch excitedly exclaimed: "Christ, Howard, I have never heard such foul language in such a short space of time. Early mornings don't suit him do they? I nearly pissed myself laughing."

Howard, wiping the tears from his eyes agreed, "Fuck me Dutch, he must be lonely in that cab he was not only swearing but talking to himself at the same time! My chest and stomach caused me grief when I was trying not to laugh. We were lucky not to blow it. We better get ourselves sorted out in case we get further visitors."

Both continued to discuss the incident in whispers when shortly after they heard quiet voices outside. They braced themselves ready for action, when the door slowly opened letting in shards of early morning daylight.

From what they could make out there were two men, who from their whispered conversation, accompanied by a rustling sound were selecting items and placing them into plastic bags.

Knowing that the intruders were not in the habit of stealing an excessive amount, Howard and Dutch together forcefully pushed down their barrier and hurried towards the thieves, shouting as they did so, which caused both surprised intruders to immediately respond by shrieking equally as loud. In the faint light of the partially open-door Dutch could see both men frozen to the spot, overwhelmed by the military style shock and awe tactics. As planned, Howard hit the light switch while Dutch closed the door preventing escape. Before them were two youths in their late teens, both unkempt and scruffily dressed, one of whom was holding a black plastic bin bag. Both looked extremely shocked, one was panting heavily and holding his hand on his chest, whilst the other appeared to be unsteady on his feet and about to pass out. Both asked if they could sit on the floor to recover from their sudden shock.

Having retrieved two loaves of bread and three boxes of cakes from their bag, which they estimated had a value of seven pounds, Howard and Dutch questioned the compliant youths as to their criminal behaviour.

The two gave their names as Mark and Jez, and fully admitted that they knew that they were doing wrong but were stealing to survive. They explained that due to problems within each of their families they had taken up residence in a dilapidated caravan in the grounds of a house where Mark's disabled uncle lived alone. The deal was that they could stay there and use his bathroom if they helped in his care. Both were unemployed so there was little money for food which was the reason for them taking the items.

They readily admitted the previous thefts which started on moving into the caravan, when they noticed that the bread delivery lorry woke them as it drove noisily passed in the early hours. Having guessed that it delivered to the supermarket, they had taken a look around and discovered the insecure storeroom. With this knowledge, if they needed food they would wait for the truck to pass the caravan before visiting the storeroom and helping themselves. They both confirmed Tony's suspicion that they only did it every other day, taking only what they needed for the three of them in the hope that the thefts would go undetected.

Despite their appearance and current dilemma, Dutch found them to be both polite and pleasant individuals and had great empathy with them as he had also been caught stealing food together with his brother Roy when a hungry and disadvantaged ten-year-old. He had not been so fortunate and was arrested for his crime. It had been one of many incidents that had caused both he and his siblings to be split up from the care of their grandparents.

Neither Howard or Dutch knew exactly how to proceed as although they did not wish to compromise the group, they had to honour what action Tony, being the aggrieved party wished to take. Howard rang Tony's mobile and the weary looking manager arrived in the loading bay within ten minutes of the call. Dutch met him outside the storeroom and informed him of what had taken place and the circumstances of the two involved. Dutch relayed the facts in a manner designed to persuade the manager to pursue some form of action that would not involve the police. He explained that, understandably, neither of the captors wished to attend any court proceedings, and both apparently destitute youths, cooperative throughout, had been given the shock of their lives. Dutch emphasised that they would never forget their capture, but still required some form of punishment.

After giving the circumstances a little thought, Tony entered the storeroom. Once inside, Howard introduced Tony to the young villains, whom Tony recognised having regularly seen them idling about the shopping parade. He confirmed that, as they had been cooperative and admitted all of the thefts, he was willing to give them a chance, and not involve the police. His conditions were that as he was short of staff he would not take action if both completed unpaid work in and around the loading bay until he was satisfied that they had paid sufficient recompense for the estimated value of all of the goods that they had stolen.

Both were agreeable and apologetic as to their conduct and very relieved as they each admitted previous minor brushes with the law.

Tony then went into conversation with Mark and Jez making arrangements for their unofficial community service, consisting of the removal of graffiti, litter picking, recycling shop waste, and repairing broken trollies. Dutch then sternly read them the riot act, stressing that there would be repercussions if they did not fulfil their commitment to Tony. In addition, their lenient treatment was conditional on them not mentioning the incident to anyone and not to informing anybody of the insecure store, with the promise that details of their thefts and any further transgressions would be passed to the police. Before leaving the store Dutch again, as with the knicker thief, took incriminating photographs of both miscreants with their intended haul.

On arrival home, Dutch decided that although he could possibly catch a couple of hours sleep, his arrival in the bedroom would probably wake Melanie. With the thoughts of both the excitement of the catch and the hilarious comments made by the driver still running through his head, he decided that sleep would be impossible anyway, so instead he took Jodie for a long leisurely walk.

On his return Melanie was awake and eager to know the result of his toils, and after Dutch relayed the full story she commented:

"It seems as if those two have got away quiet lightly as far as punishment goes."

"Yes, I suppose they have, but it was the perfect result as far as our group are concerned. They certainly fared better then Roy and me when we got caught doing a similar thing. Mind you, the disruption that it caused worked out well for me in the end."

"Of course, it did, as if that hadn't happened you may have never met me."

"The jury's still out on that one!"

In response to his quip Melanie gently punched him on his shoulder.

"Do you know Mel, those two will never forget that moment of complete silence and total darkness in that confined storeroom, when all of a sudden boxes came raining down on them from all directions and the two of us sprung out of nowhere acting like screaming banshees. They were both petrified, and it looked like the one named Jez was about to have a heart attack. I can't imagine that they would ever lurk near that storeroom at night again. And I wouldn't be at all surprised if they both spent the rest of their lives with a light on at night!"

"Perhaps I was wrong it sounds as if that alone was nearly enough punishment." Melanie sighed.

"As Howard said, our shouting and them screaming back in surprise in the pitch black came close to traumatising us as well."

....

It was early afternoon, only days after the incident when, having completed his last tour of the day, Dutch took the opportunity to call Ross to enquire if he or any of the group were at the airsoft site. Receiving the affirmative reply wished for, he drove to the site via the minor roads in the hope that at last he may be able to participate in some of the activities that Ross had previously offered.

On arrival Ross greeted him with great enthusiasm, congratulating him on his most recent result, causing Dutch to comment:

"I must say that if I hadn't joined the group I would never have thought that so much crime went on here."

"Don't be fooled Dutch. It's not that bad, it's just that you have been extremely lucky with the two jobs that you have been involved with, and we are all envious of the exceptional results - the best we've had for a long time. Like the paratrooper that you once were, you've hit the ground running."

"The jumps weren't always perfect; I've landed in my fair share of trees. As far as luck goes, I didn't logo my bus with that name for nothing."

"As I've mentioned before, most of the crime committed around here is low level stuff. But, having said that we've had our share of macabre crime in the past. Have you ever heard of the cases termed The Ladies of the Lakes?"

"No, I can't say that I have but I would be interested in case it's something I can tell my punters about."

"The first incident came to notice during the early eighties when an amateur diver discovered a body in Wast Water lake. At first it was thought to be a French female student who had been reported missing whilst fell walking in the area. But the corpse was later identified as the wife of a pilot from Surrey, who later admitted strangling her during a heated argument some eight years previously. As he went to school in Keswick and knew the lake well, he drove the body all the way up here, but he didn't know it as well as he thought, because it transpired that if he had rowed the inflatable dingy just ten yards further out into the lake the weighted body would have sunk beyond normal diving depths, the three mile long lake being the deepest in England, at over two hundred and fifty feet. Unfortunately, the student's body was found a couple of months later on the slopes of the fells and no official cause of her death had ever been given."

"I didn't know that. I have done a lot of running around the fells there, but due to the limited road access I don't usually take the bus up there unless I get a specific request."

"In the late eighties, it was amateur divers again that found a woman's body in Crummock Water. Believe it or not, it had been weighed down by an engine block. If I remember correctly she was from Leeds and her husband was convicted of her murder. I believe that it was just before the turn of the century when a third body was found in Coniston Water. It had been immersed there for a considerable time and it was many years later when her husband who was from Barrow was convicted of her murder. This was another case where again it was a bit of luck that the body was found as it landed on an underwater ledge where it was once again discovered by amateur divers."

"Blimey Ross, the divers are kept busy up here aren't they?"

"The water in the Lake District attracts the diving fraternity and we had a diver join the group, who recovered some stolen goods and articles involved in crime. The problem was he once went diving at night alone and got into severe difficulties when getting well and truly entangled in weed and underwater debris, resulting in his wife putting the mockers on him doing any more dives for us."

"What was noticeable in what you said was if the bodies had sunk to the maximum possible depths in each lake they would probably never have been discovered, which begs the question of how many more bodies may remain under the surfaces of any of the lakes?"

"That's a question us residents have all asked ourselves since these cases came to notice. You can't help to think there may be more."

"I don't think I'm going to mention any of these tales to my tourists as it may well spoil their experience. Some facts are best left unsaid."

"Right that's your lesson for today matey, what do you want to do next?"

"Basically, everything. I would like to start with having a spin around the course in a 4X4?"

"Help yourself the keys are in it and you know where to go."

Dutch spent an exciting couple of hours participating in all of the facilities available, only stopping when Ross informed him that he was securing the site for the night.

CHAPTER 6

If I Ever Lose My Faith in You *(1993)*

Written and Performed by Sting

Despite him having committed the most heinous crimes to protect and avenge his wife's tormentors, Dutch's regard for law and order and his great respect for the British Police still endured. During his worldly travels, in general, apart from the odd few, they stood far and above any other law enforcers that he had seen. But his faith in their administration of justice was shattered one afternoon while walking to his local shop, when noticing a group of youths dressed in school uniform walking towards him on the pavement. His attention was drawn to the larger and older teenager who had each of his arms wrapped tightly around the necks of two smaller younger boys. The two enveloped in the headlocks were protesting loudly and pleading to be released. As the aggressor got closer Dutch could hear one of the victims crying, so he immediately told the lad to release them both. Refusing to do so, with much bravado in the presence of his friends the boy told Dutch that it was nothing to do with him and continued walking forward still tightly gripping both distressed captives.

Dutch warned him that if he didn't release them then he would make him do so, but again he refused. Dutch was concerned about the wellbeing of the pair as he could only see the top of their heads, as their faces being enveloped between the body and coat of the assailant giving them little room to breathe. After his third request was again rejected, Dutch grabbed the youth, placing him in an head lock, which promptly resulted in the simultaneous release of the two boys, who immediately ran off. Visibly embarrassed in the presence of his school friends, the flushed youth walked away after threatening Dutch with some form of redress.

Dutch continued to the nearby shop and after only a few minutes inside, the youth's irate mother strode up, shouting and swearing, and stating that she had called the police regarding his assault of her son. Between the abuse thrown at him Dutch tried to explain the reason for his intervention, but the woman was not interested in his side of the story. With seemingly nothing to be concerned about, and thinking that he had taken the only procedure open to him rather than walking by, Dutch waited outside the shop for the police to attend. A young constable arrived, listened to all parties, and much to Dutch's surprise, he was told that the facts would be reported, and a decision would be made as to whether any formal action was to be taken against him. Following the conversation Dutch felt somewhat bemused as he thought he had done the correct thing, but now faced possible prosecution.

He asked the policeman what alternative action he might have taken, but received no reply from the constable.

A few weeks later Dutch took a telephone call from the officer concerned, who had been advised that it was an appropriate case for him to receive a verbal warning. After listening to what the officer had to say, Dutch was obliged to end the call quickly as was furious and might have said something he would later regret. The decision became even harder to accept when he was later thanked by the mother of one of the boys who informed him that she had taken her son to the doctors immediately after the incident as he complained of an injury to his neck. He was even further frustrated when he discovered that the youth responsible, who he had not hurt, had been given the same verbal caution as himself. Dutch had an intense hatred of bullies, and although he didn't consider that one so young should be severely punished, he certainly did not feel that he should have received equal admonishment himself. After all, he had rescued the two younger boys without causing any harm.

What Dutch did not realise at the time, was that the adverse decision would soon allow a more serious crime go unpunished.

Dutch bemoaned to all who would listen about his bewilderment of the judgement made against him. Then, one evening whilst cycling he came across three youths standing on a path next to the footbridge that he was about to cross. As he drew closer to them they all appeared concerned regarding his presence, raising the initial thought that perhaps they were dealing or smoking drugs, and one of the three looked so uncomfortable that Dutch considered stopping to enquire whether all was well. But such an idea soon disappeared when he contemplated what may happen if there was no problem, as it could appear, as far as the law was concerned that his intervention could again be judged unwarranted. If the situation again turned violent so soon after his last altercation, he had no faith that his good intentions would be so regarded, leaving him wide open for far worse than a verbal warning. For once in his life he ignored his hunch and continued his journey.

However, a few days later when reading the local newspaper, Dutch nearly blew a gasket, reading of a youth being mugged at knifepoint for his phone and money at the footbridge. The time and date coincided with his presence. He was though, pleased to read that the victim was not injured, and he was glad that he could not add any further details to the descriptions already known about the offenders, the incident making him even more resentful of his caution and reluctant to become further involved.

Dutch was so frustrated with the predicament that had caused him to make the wrong decision that, he informed Ross of how disillusioned he was and suggested that he temporarily stood down from any forthcoming assignments until he was in a better frame of mind.

Dutch explained "I realise that not everyone would understand my negative feelings about this, but for twenty-five years I was trained to confront danger, not shy away from it. I wish that I had seen the knife then I would have realised that I would have been fully justified to steam in. That poor lad was too frightened about being stabbed to shout out to me and must have been praying I would see the signs and intervene, but I let him down and I can't get over that. I saw the fear in his eyes and should have just followed my instincts."

Ross tried to reassure him, saying: "I fully understand how you feel but you didn't see a knife, so you had no idea what was going on. Let's say it was just three lads who resented you being suspicious of them and it turned nasty, judging by your recent dealings with the police you could have been in trouble again. Its bad decisions like that which make people resentful and mistrustful of the police, and then they don't bother to report crime, so that's another reason for our organisation to exist. I'm sure your normal service will resume as soon as possible."

"Don't worry I will bounce back once I get over the disappointment in both the police decision and myself. I have not turned anti police, but they need to encourage people to help, not dissuade as in my case, alienating public good will. I didn't expect a pat on the back, but neither did I deserve an official bollocking."

"I respect your decision to take a step back for a while, Dutch, but it would be good if you could still attend the meetings and get down to the site from time to time. How come you get all this action? Since you've been with us it's been like living in the Bronx rather than one of the most tranquil places on earth!"

"I must admit It does seem a bit that way. I have had more than my fair share of luck during my life, but I seem to get an equal share of trouble, too. Mind you some of the things I've done in the past haven't helped."

"I'm sure that applies to most of us, buddy."

Dutch couldn't say so, but thought to himself, very few had accomplished as much as him to cause the persistent threat that dogged him.

CHAPTER 7

I Started a Joke (1968)

Artists: Bee Gees
Writers: Barry, Robin and Maurice Gibb

Dutch felt somewhat obliged to answer the call for assistance from his friend Peter Bidmead, as it was him who had volunteered to teach him the art of dry-stone walling soon after arrival in the district. The possession of such a skill gave Dutch an additional income in an area designated by such barriers. He would mainly help Peter in the winter months when his tour business was slow, but on this occasion Peter was desperate for his help to quickly repair a wall struck by a lorry. With no other convenient field available for the flock of sheep, there was a danger of the animals escaping onto the road.

Once he had dropped his last passenger off from his only pre booked tour of the day, Dutch made his way to Pete's location.

It was a hot day, and both men had been at the mercy of the blazing sun for several hours. Once the work had been completed Peter proceeded to another scheduled work commitment, leaving Dutch to find a little shade, and take a much-needed drink while admiring the spectacular view spread out before him. As he pondered if it was worth plying for another tour that afternoon, his mobile rang. The phone indicated an unidentified caller so he presumed it was a potential customer who may have read one of his leaflets or media adverts.

"Good afternoon, Lucky's Lakeland Tours how may I help?"

"Hello Dennis, its Kerry are you free to talk? I have a problem and I'm hoping you may have a solution."

Dutch's thoughts went into overdrive, Kerry was the only other woman he had slept with during his marriage to Melanie. Their one-night sexual encounter occurred following meeting in a Warrington pub when Dutch was a young soldier out on a stag night. They had not seen each other since until an impromptu meeting during the previous year while Kerry was visiting the Lakes with members of her staff. During their brief conversation Kerry intimated that he was possibly the father of her twenty-year-old son, Andrew. The matter of parentage was not fully discussed as neither wished the matter to interfere with either of their happy, settled family lives. As much as Dutch always wanted to have children and would have been pleased to share in Andy's life, he knew that such news would be devastating for Melanie who was not only unaware of his infidelity, but unable to bear children.

Such an unexpected call had flustered the usually calm and collected Dutch, but in an attempt to bury his immediately worrying thoughts, he replied in a pleasant and a confident tone, "Kerry, this is a surprise. To what do I owe this pleasure?"

"I'm sorry to call you out of the blue, but I had to wait for the right opportunity when the family were not around. It was just fortunate that I remembered the name of your business and was then able to get your number from the internet. You are the only person that I can speak to about this."

Dutch was intrigued as to her comment but strongly suspected that it must concern Andrew, as after twenty years apart this was the only topic that they had in common. He sincerely hoped that her husband, from whom she had been estranged at the time of their brief affair, had not discovered that perhaps his fatherhood was in doubt.

He continued to disguise his concern by confidently replying "Fire away then Kerry, you've caught me at a good time."

"It may not be a good time for either of us unless I can solve this particular problem. In time it may directly involve you."

Dutch couldn't help himself by swiftly interjecting, "I can only think that this concerns Andy. Don't say that your husband has somehow found out about our brief relationship?"

"No not yet, but he might if Andy's best friend has anything to do with it."

"What an earth can his friend know about us?"

"He doesn't yet, but he may do if he gets what he wants Andrew to do for him. That may cause us a problem. Let me explain: Andrew has recently graduated from Loughborough University and is now a full-time professional athlete. His friend, who is still studying sports science there, is working on a dissertation to discover if certain genes can be identified from the parents of outstanding athletes, which could in future contribute towards producing super athletes. His idea is to obtain the information from blood samples taken from the athletes and their biological parents. Andrew has asked both my husband Gerry and myself if we are willing to assist his friend in his research. Andrew is keen to help, and Gerry is not concerned one way or the other, leaving me to make the final decision. I am now under pressure to give our consent to take part, but, if I do there is a risk that the research may reveal that Gerry is not Andy's father. I'm not sure that this could happen, or whether they would even disclose the fact if it did, but I can't afford to take the chance, so I need a good reason to explain to Andy as to why I don't want to provide blood. I'm not certain which of you is Andrew's father but due to his birthdate, his identical looks, and the fact that he is an excellent runner, all point to you rather than Gerry. I would have tried the excuse that I don't like needles or the sight of blood but he knows that I have voluntarily given blood in the past. I have stalled him for the moment but I need some ideas as this could possibly cause both us and our families problems should this go ahead. Any suggestions how I get out of this situation without upsetting Andy, his friend, and maintaining our little secret?"

An equally concerned Dutch momentarily paused for thought as he analysed the bombshell that Kerry had suddenly dropped on him.

He then responded, "I sympathise with your predicament, of course, and agree with your concerns. As much as I would wish to have a son, as my wife Melanie has been unable to have children no good would come of this if I were proved to be Andrew's father. You could always give as an excuse that, if the blood samples were not strictly monitored, they could cause many problems if they were to get mixed up, or failed to be destroyed. This could easily happen in an unsupervised environment such as a university. If you have a minute I can give you an example of a similar problem that happened to me"

"Yes please, go on I'm all ears, I will need examples to make a reasonable excuse not to be involved."

"As a young soldier, I was sent on a residential course. On the first day, which was the Monday, the instructors surprised us with a drink/drugs test. It was common place to have a urine test, but this time they required a blood test as it gives more results for banned substances, and was obviously carried out immediately after our weekend leave to establish whether any of us had been taking drugs or drinking heavily, and were still under the influence of either, which was a reasonable request considering that we would be handling firearms."

"Of course, in that job you have no choice but to agree to the testing and once the bloods were taken we were told that the results would be back by the end of the week. I was fully confident that I would be clear, as you will remember from when we first met that I hardly drink alcohol and certainly don't take, and never have taken, any illegal drugs."

"Yes, I know," said Kerry.

Dutch continued, "Anyway, Friday afternoon came and the class was dismissed apart from me and another male soldier. We were both then told to report to the senior officer of the training facility. I was called in first and was astounded by what I was told. He asked me if I had a drink problem, or if my previous weekend's excessive drinking was a one off. I was flabbergasted as I had a race on the Sunday before the test, so as usual I didn't have any drink at all that weekend. As much as I protested he didn't believe me, and told me apart from the alcohol I had further anomalies within my sample, and that I should immediately see my GP as, if I was telling the truth, I must have an underlying problem.

I vaguely knew the other soldier who followed me in but I waited for him to exit to see what had been said to him. He told me that he hadn't been drinking excessively that weekend either, but was told that his blood result showed otherwise and was equally as upset as me about the outcome.

"We were both allowed leave on the following Monday to see a GP and get hospital blood tests. Within days I received the result that said my blood was normal and showed no obvious medical problems. As I had not been drinking and the new test showed that I had no deficiencies in my blood system, I knew that the Army blood test result was wrong. I was inquisitive about the other soldier's hospital result and discovered that he too was given a clean bill of health. As he, like myself had not been drinking heavily the previous weekend he also could not understand why the results showed otherwise. We both sent copies of our hospital tests to the training unit, but neither of us ever heard any more about the matter."

Kerry interrupted suddenly," Christ Dennis I said I wanted an excuse, not for you to read me a bedtime story!"

"Be patient, here comes the point to this, and how dangerous it can be to leave blood samples unsupervised.

The episode remained a mystery until, years later, by chance I met with a soldier who had attended the same course, but had left the army soon after to work abroad.

"We were laughing and joking about the job in general, when suddenly, out of the blue, he told me that he and another on the course named Dave, both heavy drinkers, had consumed at lot of alcohol over that entire weekend; so, to avoid problems for themselves they conspired to randomly swap the identification labels on the blood samples taken. He found it hilarious and had forgotten that it had been me that had been given the problem to explain away. He apologised for what he thought of as a joke at the time, but I left him in no uncertainty that neither I nor the other soldier involved had found it at all amusing."

Kerry again intervened," That's a good example that I can give. I think that will also put some doubt in Gerry's mind as to why not to do it."

"But Kerry, that's not the finish of the story and it has a tragic ending. Dave the other soldier involved in the prank, who I knew reasonably well became ill several months after the course. I did happen to see him out and about at one time and he had a yellowish pallor, and his eyes didn't look at all right. It wasn't long after that I discovered that he was in hospital, terminally ill with leukaemia. I tried to see him but he wouldn't except any visitors and eventually died there."

"Now I don't know if it would have made the slightest bit of difference if he hadn't swapped his sample, with I'm guessing mine, as I was the one identified as apparently having been drinking, and also had the abnormalities in the blood. If the swap hadn't been made, it would have been

Dave who would have had the hospital test, and maybe the leukaemia would have been diagnosed earlier. When I told the other party to the prank, as he had been overseas he was unaware of Dave's death and was remorseful. I don't blame him for the tragic outcome as it was a joint decision by a couple of young men looking after their own skins, having what they thought was a laugh at the time."

"Oh, that's so tragic as to how a simple prank can backfire on you."

"If I haven't bored you too much there are other scenarios that you can put to them."

"Go on then, you are doing well so far."

"Can you imagine Kerry, that if such research did eventually discover compatible couples to produce the ultimate sportsmen and sports women, such products would rule every sport, whereby the normal everyday athlete would have no chance in competition. It would divide the sporting world into two groups of super athletes and the also rans. It would be a step too far. The authorities have already had enough problems in the past trying to adjudicate whether some female athletes' testosterone levels were too high for them to compete in women's events. Can you imagine the turmoil that designer or test tube sportsmen and women would cause? I know this is farfetched but is another spanner to throw into the works. What if any of your blood samples got into the wrong hands and left at a scene of a crime?"

"Thanks Dennis, you have given me more than enough ammunition to argue my case for not wishing to be involved in something that may lead to an unethical outcome."

"I really hope for all our sakes that you can put a stop to it as there may be a chance of releasing the cat out of the bag if what you suspect is true about the possibility of Andy being my son. In the circumstances, it's probably best for all concerned not to discuss that particular subject any further. Anyway, moving on how are you all?"

"We are all fine. Have you been following Andy's career?"

"Yes, I'm continually checking on his performances on the power of ten website and watch any athletics event on TV that he may be competing in. Let's just hope that he makes the next Olympic marathon squad."

There was a sudden break in the conversation as it became very obvious to both parties that it was becoming increasingly difficult to discuss Andrew any further without revealing both their emotions and regrets.

Kerry broke the silence, "Well look after yourself, Dennis. I will let you know if I have any further scares like this as I may need your advice again."

"Best of luck with everything Kerry, bye."

Dutch remained sitting and contemplating, as once again Kerry had further suggested that Andrew may be his son, the son that he had always wished for, but could never claim without causing misery and upset to others.

His negative thoughts were interrupted when Melanie called him wishing to know what time he would be home for his tea.

CHAPTER 8

Sunday Bloody Sunday *(1983)*

Artists: U2
Writers: U2

As weeks passed since Kerry's distressed call, Dutch felt sure that as he had heard nothing further she had hopefully derailed the students request.

It was a beautiful sunny morning when he picked up a group of Japanese tourists for a full day trip. Just as he had planned, he reached the beauty spot of Tarn Hows, just two miles northeast of Lake Coniston in time to allow the visitors to have their lunch and explore the special views over the Lakeland fells. After handing out his self-produced guided map of the popular circular walk of the lake and accentuating to the English-speaking leader of the group to keep to the designated paths, he further explained that the Tarns were so named as they were the smaller mountain lakes of the area, situated in hollows, surrounded by steep slopes formed by glaciers.

Dutch was well aware from previous tours that the group should complete the walk in just over an hour in which time he would have his lunch, listen to the radio and converse with any other waiting drivers. Many of the larger coaches would provide a guide to accompany their parties on the walk, but Dutch could see little point as the circular path was well worn and well-marked. The magnificent scenery spoke for itself and as only a couple of the twelve strong group spoke English, would make most of any commentary that he could provide would be pointless.

As he was eating he noticed that one of the English speaking passengers had left a daily newspaper on their seat.

He was not one to often read a tabloid newspaper but with time on his hands he picked it up and on flicking through the pages his attention became focused on an article headed 'Soldier F case adjourned until next month'. Due to his previous military service he had been following the case with great interest. The infamous incident originated from a violent clash between members of the 1st Battalion Parachute Regiment and civil rights demonstrators in the Bogside – a predominantly Catholic part of Londonderry, Northern Ireland on Sunday,30th January 1972 widely known as Bloody Sunday. Thirteen demonstrators were killed and fifteen injured when the troops, after apparently coming under fire themselves, fired on the large crowd. The incident was widely criticized and an enquiry was held which largely cleared the soldiers responsible, but described the soldiers shooting as "bordering on the reckless". However, it was announced in March 2019, some 47 years following the event that there was enough evidence to prosecute the 66-year-old Soldier F for two murders and five further charges of attempted murder.

Despite the rights and wrongs of the long-standing political unrest in Northern Ireland, Dutch had a personal interest in the situation, not only as a former paratrooper himself, but it was as a result of the continuing troubles that his own father was killed in the same province two years after Bloody Sunday.

Paratrooper, Corporal Dennis French had been standing in the rain outside a house in the small village of Crossmaglen, South Armagh, locally referred to as bandit country due to its reputation for lawlessness. The soldier was vigilantly guarding local police officers and colleagues searching what was suspected of being a property used as a weapons store. The street that he was patrolling was one in an area known as sniper's alley and its reputation proved accurate as the soldier was shot in the neck and died instantly.

It was his death that ultimately caused his wife Sadie, with her four young children and another to be born, who would carry her husband's name, to become increasingly depressed.

Born slightly prematurely, young Dennis was scant consolation to his already distraught mother, and the tragedy of her husband's death was further compounded when she discovered that the family were required to vacate their army accommodation. Dennis, the youngest of the five children moved with his mother and siblings to their new home in Brighton, Sussex close to her parents Connie, and her fisherman husband, nicknamed Sinbad. Despite the move to the coast, Sadie, with increasing financial problems and feeling unable to cope with her husband's death while bringing up the children alone, rapidly descended into deeper despair and when Dennis was only five she took her own life leaving her orphaned children to be cared for by her parents.

Although all five children were truly loved by their grandparents, lack of finances and opportunities, plus all of them being regularly bullied caused Dennis and his brother Roy to become unruly and gain unwanted attention from the authorities.

Because of the deteriorating family situation, at the age of ten, Dennis and his siblings were distributed among other family members. Dennis went to live with his aunt and uncle in Hampshire, proving to be a vastly beneficial move altering the course of his life, especially when pursuing a career in the Army.

Due to the circumstances of his father's premature death ultimately causing such devastation to his entire family, Dennis inherited an intense bitterness for the terrorist group responsible. Yet, years later, during his seven operational tours of Northern Ireland, known as operation Banner, he had been present in equally ferocious riots as those of bloody Sunday, but despite intense provocation, always remained conscious that he could not let his deeply felt emotions jeopardise what he intended to be a lifetime career.

Having been confronted with such perilous situations himself, Dutch fervently opposed decisions made by politicians and others in the judicial system to charge soldier F so long after the event. Most if not all, of those responsible for the decision to prosecute, had never been in the violent world of a riot, and they had never experienced the ill feelings one gets when confronted by a violent mob.

Although before his time, he did not believe that the march on 30th January,1972 was a peaceful demonstration, as some had described, as the news clips of that day showed brick-strewn roads and petrol bombs being thrown. Numerous piles of prepared supplies of bricks, rubble, petrol, and nail bombs were later discovered, showing that the intentions of many of those present were far from peaceful. His personal view was if you play with fire then you can expect to be burnt. He did not believe that any soldier deliberately sets out on any patrol with an intention of killing innocent people in cold blood, but those involved in a riot like the Bloody Sunday incident were there to hurt, injure, maim, or kill soldiers.

He was aware that the terrorist tactics during those times were to form a crowd or demonstration which would require soldiers to monitor the situation. Having placed their gunmen in prepared locations, agitators would then stir the crowd from within, who on the given word would suddenly disperse leaving the soldiers at the mercy of the gunmen.

Dutch, as one of the many soldiers who served through the operation banner campaign was appalled at many of the decisions made by the 1998 Good Friday agreement which allowed more than 200 terrorist suspects to be given freedom assurances, while members of the UK security forces were left exposed to prosecution, as in the case of soldier F. It was no wonder that British army veterans felt betrayed by successive governments, when known previously convicted murderous terrorists are allowed to walk around scot free.

Such thoughts of what he considered was a 'sell out' made Dutch's blood boil.

In the same column the article added that the high-profile case had attracted further historic claims from other parts of the world, accusing British troops of atrocities.

This passage slightly concerned Dutch, as serving as part of a NATO (North Atlantic Treaty Organization), peace keeping force during the Kosovo war in the late nineties, when leading a small group of soldiers at night in pursuit of rebel forces, an event occurred which subjected him to the first of only two disciplinary investigations of his entire career. A heavily armed military breakaway group were responsible for pillaging a village, committing terrible atrocities of murder and rape of both women and children. When Dutch and his squad caught up with the small band of rebels, one made an attempt to fire his weapon whilst another lunged for a grenade attached to his belt, causing the patrol, including Dutch, to open fire on the entire group, resulting in all six men being killed.

When the report of the incident reached higher command there was suspicion that some of the rebels could have been captured alive. In the eyes of all the soldiers involved, this was not the case, as having seen at least two of the rebels in the tightly packed group move towards weapons their immediate response was to protect themselves and their colleagues, and to immediately stop the threat by strafing the group with automatic fire. The incident was thoroughly investigated, but as it was proved that all of the deceased were heavily armed and all of the civilian victims refused to co-operate with the investigating officers, beyond praising their liberators, no further action was taken. It was from this campaign that Dutch was able to smuggle a Walther pistol with ammunition into the UK, which he considered to be a war trophy, which he hid and later used to shoot and kill the two responsible for raping his wife.

Soon afterwards, to avoid detection he disposed of the weapon in a tidal river but since the recent threat to his life wished he were still in possession of the gun.

Although the newspaper report had made him consider that the incident could be reviewed, he felt confident that it would not be the case, as there were no other witnesses apart from the soldiers themselves. But he was aware that there was always the possibility of spurious witnesses emerging from the woodwork, with a grievance or compensation in mind. After all soldier F could not have expected to stand trial all those years later, making any similar proceedings possible, regardless of when or where they had occurred.

The second, and only other serious disciplinary proceedings that Dutch had faced in his twenty-five-year army career took place whilst serving in Northern Ireland. Dutch had been assigned with a colleague named Chris to drive an armoured Land Rover to assist the police at a temporary vehicle check point, with a view to stopping any wanted terrorists or undercovering the transport of any arms or bomb making equipment.

Chris and Dutch were both armed and closely observing their police colleagues as they engaged in searching vehicles and their occupants. Then, one of the officers alerted the entire search team that a stolen vehicle was being pursued by other police officers and was being driven so recklessly that all of the passengers had bailed out of the moving car. The stolen vehicle was heading straight towards their position and was at a location where there were no further turnings for the offender to avoid the checkpoint. It was immediately decided that the vehicle must be stopped before a serious accident occurred. The police inspector in charge instructed that three police vehicles be positioned across the road to force the car to stop. Once the vehicles were in place all of the uniformed officers waited behind the barricade with weapons at the ready in case the driver was armed. After only a short time a silver Vauxhall motor car came into their view as it negotiated a left-hand bend at high speed, shortly followed by a marked police vehicle. On seeing the obstruction placed before him the Vauxhall driver braked hard and due to its speed the vehicle skidded off of the road surface into a grass bank and the surrounding thick hedge. The driver proceeded to try to drive on but the bank and bushes made it impossible for the saloon car to proceed. Unable to move the vehicle and circled by police officers, a youth left the car, jumped onto the bonnet, leapt over the hedge, and continued running across the large field of rough ground. He was immediately pursued by the police officers, but was very fast on his feet and it was obvious to the soldiers that the officers would not catch him on foot so, both Chris and Dutch instinctively entered their Land Rover and after a few attempts the robust vehicle climbed the perimeter bank, crashing through the dense hedge into the field. Dutch drove across the undulating terrain at high speed attempting to avoid as many potholes as possible, causing a most uncomfortable ride for both men. As they closed in on the fleeing youth Dutch would have normally been confident in his fitness and running ability to make the catch, but the youth was heading straight for a robust wire fence situated at the foot of a railway embankment. Not relishing the thought of negotiating the fence and chasing him along a busy live railway track, Dutch drove alongside the youth until both pursuer and miscreant were level, he then forcibly pushed open his door, which, with the forward motion of the Land Rover swung open and striking the youth violently across his back, causing him to shriek loudly as he was projected forward and off his feet. Chris's immediate response was to loudly exclaim in a concerned tone, "Christ Dutch, I hope you haven't killed him?" On stopping the vehicle Dutch hurriedly approached the motionless youth who was lying flat on his face on the dusty surface. Alarm bells momentarily rang in his head, heightened by the thought of Chris' exclamation. As Dutch reached the prone individual he began to struggle to his feet, at the same time panting heavily and complaining of being winded with pain in his back.

Both Chris and Dutch both supported and restrained the unsteady youth for a short time until the arrival of the police officers, who then took him into custody. Both soldiers made statements to the police, expecting that to be the end of the matter.

It was however only a few weeks later that Dutch was called into a police station for "further enquiries". Once there, he learnt that despite the youth not being seriously injured, and despite having been charged with theft of a vehicle, reckless driving, and various other motoring offences, causing injuries to others escaping from the speeding vehicle, his father had made a complaint of assault.

Dutch's explanation to both the police and military investigations were that he was about to stop the vehicle and give chase on foot and had prematurely partly opened his door when the wind caused it to fly open, in turn hitting the youth, accidently knocking him off of his feet. His explanation was corroborated by his colleague Chris, bringing the matter to a close. Dutch never regretted his actions but was thankful that he had not caused serious injury. He also hoped that the youth concerned would have learnt a painful lesson before considering a return to crime.

Although he had only just arrived home from a long day's work, Dutch was quite content to answer Melanie's call for assistance with her larger than usual shopping list. Having made the excuse of his many commitments, he had managed to swerve shopping for a considerable time, so a trip to Sugden's supermarket would not only appease his wife but also give him the opportunity to pick up some treats for himself.

It was the first time that he had visited the supermarket since assisting in the apprehension of Jez and Mark for the thefts from the storeroom. Although pleased with the result of their intervention in the matter, he still felt aggrieved about the disappointing decision taken by the police, which ultimately prevented him from stopping a mugging. Due to his intense feelings about both matters he had still not yet regained his enthusiasm to assist Ross and the group in their neighbourhood crime busting activities.

The couple were in the process of selecting goods when they were approached by Tony the shop manager. After a friendly reunion, Tony beckoned them to leave their half full trolley and to follow him to another isle. As they entered the isle Dutch was surprised to see Jez stacking tinned goods from the contents of a trolley. On seeing Dutch, Jez greeted him with a smile and a friendly nod of the head, then continued with his work. Before any explanation was given, and acting in a secretive manner Tony asked them both to follow him to the rear of the store, where in the delivery bay Jez's partner in crime Mark, was in the process of breaking down cardboard boxes and placing the flattened material into a recycling bin. Mark, like Jez just acknowledged the three spectators with a friendly nod before resuming his task. Tony then walked them back into the store, at the same time explaining that once he had considered that both youths had completed a sufficient period of unpaid work in recompense for their crimes, having been so impressed with their enthusiasm and work ethic that he had taken them on a for a trial period with a view to offering them both part time positions. They had also solved the problem of securing the storeroom following the morning delivery, as they were alternating in rising early to lock it. However, Tony stressed that he was keeping a keen eye out for any missing stock.

After arriving home and packing away the shopping Melanie and Dutch discussed the merits of what Howard, Dutch and the organisation as a whole had achieved. As the incident had not only detected and prevented further thefts but had found useful employment for two lads who otherwise would have not been given the opportunity, diverting them from a future life of crime.

With a feeling of fulfilment and with Melanie's newly found encouragement, later that evening Dutch contacted Ross informing him that he was available for future assignments.

CHAPTER 9

Deal with the Devil *(2005)*

Artists: Judas Priest
Writers: Halford, Downing, Tipton, Roy Z

As the majority of his usual working day was spent sitting behind the wheel of his tour bus, Dutch would take every opportunity to find time to fit in either a daily cycle ride or run. He felt he had now improved his fitness enough to attempt to start breaking some age-related records at parkrun events and club contested races, over both cross country and the steep, unforgiving fells. The Tuesday evening club training run always ended with most of the athletes congregating in one of the local pubs. It was on such an evening when one of the runners was asked to compile a list of personal best recorded times for each individual athlete. When it came to Dutch's turn to reveal his feats as a younger athlete the gathering was amazed at his record over the various recognised distances. They were especially impressed by his 2-hour 18-minute time over the London marathon course. And, after the survey was complete he became somewhat embarrassed as many of the group bombarded him with numerous questions regarding training techniques, hydration, the best trainers to wear and so forth.

On seeing Dutch's discomfort, the club captain intervened, suggesting that Dutch be appointed long-distance coach, enabling him to evaluate each runner and advise them according to their ability. The motion was soon seconded and carried by the entire group giving Dutch little option but to accept the position. But, he added the proviso that he could also work with some of the younger aspiring athletes. He made the additional request as since entering the veteran ranks of the sport he had attained an ambition to create a rising star, similar to the potential British International runner Andrew Barlow, possibly his son.

It was during the general conversation that followed that Dutch was forced to leave the noisy pub to take an unidentified incoming telephone call. The caller asked if Dutch had one place available for an afternoon tour the following day.

Dutch informed the male caller that some seats had been reserved, but he could accommodate an additional passenger for the tour leaving Windermere Tourist information centre car park at 2 p.m.

The male, speaking in broken English, in an accent that Dutch could not readily recognise, informed him that as his car had broken down and requested to be picked up on his way to Windermere, continuing to explain the location where he would be waiting. Many of his clients had strong accents, so as he often did, he requested the caller to repeat the precise pick up location as, to his knowledge, the lay by that he was indicating was in a secluded area, some distance from any of the guest houses or other accommodation. The caller repeated the same location, also declining Dutch's offer that in case of any bad weather it would be beneficial to collect him from wherever he was staying. Dutch found the man vague and his request rather odd, but although he was fairly new to the tour business, he had soon become used to strange requests for assistance when dealing with all walks of life from around the globe. The conversation concluded after Dutch had tried to establish the enquirers mobile number and politely thanked him for the call.

Dutch looked at his map and remained puzzled about the location of the collection as it was so remote and made no sense, unless he was remaining overnight with the broken-down vehicle, or was obtaining a lift to the spot. But if the latter were the case why couldn't his lift continue the ten-minute journey on to Windermere? Also, why had he not taken the easy option to get collected from his accommodation as Dutch had suggested? Although this was his first full season at the job he had already experienced time wasters who had not turned at appointed times and places. When previously speaking to some of the more seasoned tour operators about peculiar occurrences, they had explained that some were just weirdos doing it for their own amusement and other bogus callers were motivated by the intense summertime competition within the business, whereby rogue operators or unlicensed tour touts would divert business competitors away from the popular areas at peak times.

Dutch considered the answers, which made him suspect that the caller might have been attempting a strange accent to make a nuisance call, or just inconveniencing him for personal reasons that he could not appreciate.

He wondered whether to ring the enquirer, but then remembered the call was made from an undisclosed number, which was even more perplexing. The circumstances left Dutch in a quandary. Should he now assume that it was a malicious call? Or, had a confused and lone foreign tourist given the number incorrectly, or had he not recorded it correctly due to the caller's accent? But, with no address and as the call was made from an unidentified number, he was unable to investigate the matter any further, and just accepted that dealing with foreign travellers was not always straight forward, so he decided that, as the lay by was not far from where he was intending to drop off the last passenger of his morning tour, he would go to the appointed spot. If the call was genuine and he left the tourist alone and stranded, he did not wish to get a further derogatory web site review to accompany the one already submitted by a woman, who whilst under the influence of drink or drugs, had caused so much disruption on a particular tour that he had been forced to eject her from his vehicle. Even though she was eventually arrested by the police, she nevertheless had the audacity to blame him for her detention, posting a damming review to harm his business.

As soon as the last of the passengers from his morning tour had departed, Dutch had a bite to eat and then decided to proceed to the lay by, as even if the caller did not appear at least he would have confirmed his suspicions and put the matter to rest.

As he approached the pick up point in his distinctive logoed minibus he saw a man standing at the side of a smart navy-blue BMW, parked on a rough layby at the side of the narrow country lane. His suspicions were heightened as Dutch considered that if the vehicle had broken down in such a remote area surely the driver would have arranged the repair or collection of the expensive car the evening before, or that morning, rather than leaving it and going on a lone jaunt around the countryside.

Dutch sensed something didn't ring true and stopped his minibus well short of the man and rear of the parked BMW. The tall, dark casually dressed male stood by the driver's door summoning Dutch by hand gestures to come to him. Dutch's first thoughts were that he may have been set up for a robbery, or the worst-case scenario that the cartel may have returned as they had indicated that they would. With these thoughts in mind he scoured the trees and hedges on either side of the lane, at the same time keeping an eye on the male who remained standing, still trying to encourage Dutch from his vehicle. He had a sense of foreboding and his gut feeling of a dangerous situation had seldom let him down in the past. So, he locked his doors and reversed, because if the lone male were armed he would be an easy target if he passed him and the BMW on the narrow lane. As he backed onto a track leading into a field, he decided despite any possible repercussions that could affect his business, he was not going to remain in the area a moment longer. As Dutch drove away he looked into his rear-view mirror and saw another male quickly emerge from the undergrowth from the opposite side of the road to the BMW and run to the car to which the driver had re-entered and was in the process of moving. Although Dutch only caught a glimpse of the running man he was certain he was holding something, possibly a handgun.

Dutch was now convinced that he had avoided an ambush. He was certain that these were members of the aggrieved criminal gang, as he thought it very unlikely that armed robbers would target a humble tour operator, not expected to be carrying a great deal of cash.

Just before negotiating a sharp right-hand bend, Dutch again took another glance into his mirror and saw the BMW being slowly turned around allowing the second man to get in. The ambush had failed, but rather than flee the scene it seemed as if they were about to pursue him, presumably to attempt to retrieve their initial plan. Dutch had visions of an assignation plot. But was he being melodramatic?

As he sped along a rare short straight section of the rural lane he observed the BMW fast approaching behind. Although his pursuers had the advantage of superior speed and road holding ability, Dutch, had extensive knowledge of most of the roads and lanes across a wide area and knew that if he could sustain a reasonable speed his followers would neither be able to overtake him or be in a position to aim an accurate gun shot. His thoughts quickly turned to how he was going to extricate himself from an apparently extremely dangerous situation. He could drive into the nearest busy town or village which may delay any attack on him as it had on their previous menacing visit, but he dismissed the idea as on this occasion they may lose patience which could lead to other casualties, such gangsters having little regard for collateral damage. Even if such a move did prevent them temporarily from taking any action, it would only be a short time before the relentless pursuit would resume, as it was unlikely that they would want to return on another occasion.

Dutch could only think of one person who may be able to help to resolve the predicament that he found himself in.

Whilst negotiating the long, winding rural lane at speeds far in excess of how he would normally drive his beloved vehicle, he reached for his phone and with difficulty used the speed dial facility which was answered over his blue tooth speaker.

"Hello Dutch, are you planning to join us this afternoon then?"

Relieved to hear his friends voice, Dutch in an unusually concerned tone replied, "I hadn't planned to Ross but I might now as I need your help urgently. I've got to make this call double quick as I'm being chased by two blokes in a blue BMW who tried to set me up, but I sussed them out. I'm sure that they are from my past and if so they'll be armed. I hate to put you in this position, but any ideas? If not I can hopefully get far enough ahead of them down the track to the site, abandon my van and leg it into the woods and work something out later."

"Can't you call the police or drive to a police station?"

"No believe me, even if they got nicked that would only stall the problem. It's not going to go away that easy."

"Fucking hell Dutch. I know you like a bit of excitement in your life but this is bloody ridiculous."

Ross paused momentarily, then resumed, "I'm in the woods at the moment with Gerry Taylor trying to bag a couple of pheasants. We've both got our shotguns so that could help. There's half a dozen of us up here at the moment so if you can give them the run around for ten minutes I will try and set something up. Drive into the car park and run up the bank and into bushes near the border control post. I'll meet you there. Got that?"

"Understood and thanks. Hopefully see you there."

After the termination of the call Dutch quickly glanced at the dashboard clock, then mentally devised a route of narrow lanes that would take approximately ten minutes to reach the site entrance in Parish lane. He continued at the highest speed possible, so as not to give the pursuers any opportunity to pass or get a decent shot at him, and consequently narrowly avoided the occasional oncoming car or mobile farm machinery. At the same time, despite the predicament that he was in, he hoped that the authorities would not receive any complaints regarding the reckless driving of his easily identifiable vehicle.

In just over ten minutes Dutch reached the track leading to the activity centre. The determined duo had not been unable to overtake him but had remained on his tail throughout. Dutch could only assume that to be so persistent they were in fear of returning to their leaders having failed to accomplish their given mission, similar to their colleague's disappointment some months earlier.

As Dutch sped down the dry, dusty, pine needle-covered track, with his knowledge of the hazards, and the plume of dust he was creating gave him enough advantage to put some distance between him and the pursuing BMW. Once he reached the car park Dutch skidded to a halt on the gravel surface and ran up the bank indicated by Ross, where he saw Ross beckoning him through a gap between some dense rhododendron bushes, which they both then crouched behind. Ross pulled on his ski mask, but before they were able to converse the BMW came sliding to a halt on the edge of the car park. It then continued slowly and cautiously forward, with both driver and front seat passenger surveying all around them through the open windows.

Ross quietly said to Dutch," We are all in place to help. We can protect you but obviously you can understand that we have to be careful how far we go with this."

"Fair enough it's my problem. I'm just very fortunate that you are here to help."

"If they are armed we have a plan of action that we have practiced in the past, but I never envisaged that our war games would ever be as beneficial as this."

Both Ross and Dutch then observed the BMW stopping close to the apparently unattended minibus and after alighting from their vehicle both men briefly looked inside and also glanced underneath the people carrier. As they did so Ross and Dutch could clearly see that they were both holding pistols close to the sides of their bodies. Following a brief discussion, the two trespassers walked towards the entrance of the airsoft site.

Ross then hurriedly commented, "I don't want them getting in the compound as there is too much cover. We need them in the open."

As soon as the words had left his mouth Ross fired a shot from his Remington Camo pump action shotgun into the canopy of branches of large nearby oak trees that overhung the car park. The multitude of discharged lead shot caused a mass of twigs and leaves to rain down on the interlopers, causing both to stop and look around, attempting to identify the firing point.

Able to observe both from behind his cover, Ross then shouted," Drop your weapons. You are both trespassing on my land with firearms so I have the right to defend myself and my property. You have been warned."

Both men looked towards each other and with guns prominently drawn, then shuffled backwards towards their vehicle, but rather than entering it and drive away, took up defensive positions from behind their car, shielding themselves from where they believed both the shot and announcement had emanated.

Ross called out again, "Final warning, throw your guns into the open."

When neither of the men responded to the order, Ross shouted a clear rehearsed signal at the top of his voice, "Geronimo" and fired another round into the trunk of another oak tree situated close to the two crouching individuals.

In an almost simultaneous response to his call another gun shot gun blast was heard coming from the opposite side of the car park to Ross and Dutch's position. The shot fired from the weapon of Gerry Taylor again hit a section of the canopy of branches bringing more debris down onto the men and the two parked vehicles. Within seconds of both salvos an arrow crashed into the rear window of the BMW causing the glass to shatter, immediately followed by another, the point of which embedded itself into the ground close behind the two gunmen.

Ross shouted once more," If you don't throw your guns away next time we will all be on target."

After shouting the warning Ross commented to Dutch who remained crouched by his side, "If they don't comply I don't know what the fuck we do next, as we can't just kill the bastards?"

"This is my fight you have all done more than enough. I can't drop you all in the shit, or even worse get you shot by these arse holes. If you give me your gun I'll take over?"

"Fair enough Dutch, I can't put these other blokes at risk of either."

With that Ross broke the shotgun and replaced the two used cartridges. After closing the weapon, he pointed out the safety catch and handed Dutch the gun together with three more new cartridges that he retrieved from his large leather game bag slung over his shoulder. Dutch carefully placed the ammunition in his pockets for easy access.

From his vantage position Dutch lay prone and aimed the gun as close as he thought was possible without hitting either the men or the vehicles in the knowledge that if they then tried to rush him, Ross's gun held three shells and he had two shots remaining to prevent their advance.

He then shouted, "Final chance" and fired the weapon just far enough above the top of their car that a small amount of shot was heard striking the metal roof.

After the loud noise from the gun had diminished, both men slowly rose up from behind the BMW, at the same throwing their pistols on the ground in front of them.

Sensing the danger of the weapons being only a short distance from their feet. Dutch Shouted, "One of you pick them up and throw them further into the centre of the car park."

It then became obvious that at least one of the two who he presumed were members of the foreign led cartel spoke English. The man he recognised from the lay by stepped forward and tossed the guns to a reasonably safe distance.

Dutch then firmly instructed them to move into open ground away from both the vehicles and the discarded guns, and to turn their pockets inside out and raise their hands. Once they had complied, following a brief conversation between Ross and Dutch they both emerged from the top of the bank. Ross was first to scramble down and collect both pistols with his gloved hands, and after activating their safety catches, confirmed to Dutch that they were genuine and fully loaded. He then placed each weapon into his bag. At the same time Dutch walked towards his pursuers, covering them with his shotgun.

With perfect timing the other group members of two archers and the shotgun toting Gerry Taylor, all wearing ski masks emerged from different points around the surrounding banks. They were soon joined by two intimidating figures dressed in camouflage battle dress and wearing NATO style helmets with visors and carrying the impressive airsoft replicas of the Heckler and Koch military assault rifles.

Ross then pursed his lips and emitted a loud shrill whistle, a signal, which caused Blitz to come bounding out from one of the huts where despite the gunshots, the dog, impervious to such common sounds had been peacefully sleeping. On reaching his master the dog obediently lay at Ross's feet, who then imitated a growl to which Blitz responded with a similar, but far more ferocious and louder snarl, at the same time curling a lip and bearing his large fearsome set of teeth. Ross then instructed the dog to stay, the animal responded by laying prone, continually staring inquisitively at the two strangers. It was clear that both men were wary of the large Rottweiler and continually kept their eyes on him, unaware that unless they attacked Ross they were more likely to be licked to death then bitten.

Ross then removed a number of thick white cable ties from his bag, and on showing them to Dutch said, "Do you want them trussed up. Neither of them looks very trustworthy?"

"Yes, best tie them up. I don't think that two blokes who were about to shoot me should be given an inch."

Ross, then with an expertise gained from his years of participating in war games, used the cable ties to handcuff the duo.

With the pair incapacitated, Ross then made a cursory search by running his hands over their clothing. After confiscating a mobile telephone from the trousers pockets of each, he then ran his hands across the trousers of the seemingly less compliant former passenger, and, as he felt the area over his left ankle, Ross momentarily halted. He then proceeded to raise the trouser leg to reveal a vicious looking knife contained in a leather sheath strapped around the calf. Ross released the knife from its holder and as he placed it in his bag with the telephones and guns looked at the passenger loudly commenting: "This one's obviously a really nasty fucker."

Dutch replied, "Yeah he looks a particularly evil piece of shit but I'd bet the other one is no better. Now they are incapable of doing fuck all, this is now down to me to sort out alone. I may need some help later depending on how things go from here on. If I could ask you to all disappear for a while I will have a little chat with these two."

Ross then instructed both captives to sit on the ground and after they had reluctantly complied he then indicated to his five colleagues to retreat into the site entrance. As he did so, he turned to Dutch, handed him the bag, and in an aggressive tone bellowed, "Just shout if you need us as we won't be far away. If it comes to it and you have to take them on a trip into the woods there is a pick and shovel available should you need it."

It was noticeable to Dutch that the comment caused both captives to look at each other with concerned expressions.

Once the group and dog were out of site Dutch addressed them both. "As you two appear to want to kill me I can only think you are from the Romanian gang that I upset years ago. Is that right?"

Neither man looked at him or replied to his comment.

This caused Dutch to aggressively respond, "Are you both understanding what I am saying? I'm not playing about here; you are in serious shit."

Both acknowledged that they understood by nodding their heads in a positively manner.

"I know that you will be in fear of your own lives if you say anything about them, but I need to know what I am dealing with to sort this out once and for all. The way I see it there are three ways that we can deal with this. The first is that I now call the police and tell them that you tried to rob me. I can give them the guns and knife, and what will you say in your defence; If you have been sent here by that firm it would certainly be better for both of you to take the wrap for an attempted robbery, rather than admitting that you were here to kill me. With my half a dozen witnesses you will be going down for a long time for both the attempt and the firearms crimes alone. Do you both understand what I have said so far?"

The driver replied in an eastern European accent "Yes, I speak the English. He also do too but not so good as me. You know who sent us and why?"

"Good, that's cleared that up, but if your surly mate is not willing to cooperate we will have to go with the worse option for you both. Let me also remind you that if you get arrested you might not survive long in jail. That ruthless gang of yours aren't going to take a chance on you doing a deal with the police for information about their little operation; So, they will have to shut you up some way or other. Is he listening? He doesn't appear interested and is making me angry. Considering that he was prepared to shoot me I will have no problems doing the same to him."

The driver then turned to his apparently mute colleague and commenced to speak in a determined manner in a foreign language, but Dutch immediately interrupted, instructing him to speak in English only.

The captive then resumed, "We must listen because you know what to expect for our failure, we have big problems with either this one or the boss."

The belligerent passenger looked at the ground and sneeringly replied in a similar accent, "Okay, I listen."

"Good. Now, as your fate is in my hands, and the second option is that I just take you into the woods, shoot you both and bury you there. I can then drive the BMW into one of our deepest lakes where it won't be found for years. I am not at all concerned about doing this. Who is going to report you missing? Think about it, is anyone going to report either of you missing, saying we last saw them when we sent them up to Cumbria to kill a man?"

Or, thirdly, better for all of us, is for me to speak with your boss to try to see if we can find a solution to sort this mess out that will satisfy us all."

The driver immediately commented: "How you think you going to speak to our boss?"

"We have your mobile phones; you must be in contact with him when your job is done here."

He sneeringly replied "You joking; what he say to us if we tell him what happened. Even if you don't kill us, we don't be able to go back there."

"Well you have a few minutes to discuss it. If you are not willing to give me your leader's details I will have to decide on one of the other bad options. But be quick because these other men have better things to do than hang around here for you two arseholes."

After a few minutes Dutch interrupted their whispered conversation by forcefully stating, "That's it, enough, I need a decision right now?"

"If we agree to give you his number what happens to us?"

"I can guarantee that he won't want me involving the police, as that would lead back to him and his syndicate So there is a good chance that we can reach some agreement. If we don't then I will have to take the best option that suits me. It's got to be in your interest for me to speak with him."

The driver looked at his colleague who again just nodded in agreement.

"Okay take out either phone, find contacts and click on Z."

Dutch removed a phone from the bag and dialled as instructed.

After a few ring tones his call was answered by a gruff foreign male voice," Luca, is it done?"

Dutch replied, "No. It's not done. Whatever you do, do not end this call, as believe me you and your two numb nuts will regret it."

"Who is this?"

"It's the man you want dead."

His comment was met by a short silence, which was then followed by, "Where are my two men?"

"They are here. They are a bit tied up at the moment and we need to talk."

"Before I speak more with you I need to speak with them."

"No problem. The call will be on loudspeaker and if you start talking anything other than English I will end the call and hand them both over to the police with their guns. If that happens your two boys will be tempted to lesser their sentence by doing a deal with the police, telling them about your organisation."

"I understand what you are saying let me speak to Luca."

Having established that Luca was the driver, Dutch switched the phone to loudspeaker, held it close to the detainee and indicated for him to speak.

"Hello."

"Luca, what the fucking hell is going on? Before you answer is there any sign of this call being recorded?"

"No, we are on my phone out in the open."

"You fucking idiots, you get sent to do something and I get this phone call. What the fuck went wrong? Be very careful what you say."

"He has an army here to protect him. You won't believe us, but it's true. If we get the chance to explain you will understand."

"This is the second time this has gone wrong. So, we do not understand. Where the hell are you now? Why aren't you trying to get away?"

"We are tied up in the woods, still somewhere in the Lake District, surrounded by men with weapons."

Dutch, still with the shotgun positioned under his arm, switched the loudspeaker off, then put the phone to his ear saying," That's enough chat. I'm assuming that you are in charge of these two. They are in a very unfavourable position at the moment, and their fate is in your hands. The best option for me right now is that I dispose of them both, but that will mean that your aim of getting me will just carry on and I'm getting fed up with that.

You obviously speak good English, so tell me why you won't stop chasing me. What I did was years ago and I had good reason. If we can't come to a ceasefire today then these two are taking a visit to the police station. Then your worries will begin."

"I don't want to discuss this matter over the phone, it's too dangerous for us both."

"I also have to be careful what I say, but it's a chance we both have to take. I'm certain that this will not be settled by us meeting in a polite chat over a cup of tea anytime soon. We will just have to be careful what words we use. I'm sure that your phones, more than most others are as safe as they can be from any interested parties."

The gang boss continued, "Perhaps. They are encrypted, but aren't you the one who's been nosey recently?"

"What do you mean by that remark?"

"We can talk about that later. As you called me I guess that there's something that you want?"

"Yes. It's called peace. I take it that you know what started all of this off?"

"I was not in that area at the time, but yes I know all of the details."

"Well, I would have thought that even someone in your game would have some understanding as to why I did what I did."

"We did understand, and even though it interrupted us for a short time, it was decided that by removing useless drunks and others who we discovered were deceiving us, in a way you saved us from doing the job. That is why we didn't bother you any further."

"What are you talking about? Dutch enquired: "Almost two years after that you had someone watching my wife, and then you sent a couple of your blokes out into the countryside to get me, but they came unstuck, just like these two here."

"Ahaa, so you thought that was us! But that was a personal vendetta by the younger brother of one of the three men that we, and the police were sure that you dealt with. Believe me I didn't know about that; it was a personal thing that was kept from me. We had no plans to bother you again but things changed."

"So, are you really telling me that you were not interested in any revenge then? So why now, what's changed? What was the previous visit about, soon after I had moved up here?"

"On that occasion you lived up to your company name as I required my men back here very quickly, so they were told to leave you and just give you a warning."

"A warning for what?"

The conversation between them was becoming stilted and increasingly difficult as both attempted not to use words to incriminate themselves in any wrong doings.

"Not many who cross us get away so lightly, but as I have already said, some could understand your anger. And even though what you did caused a lot of disruption to our business, from that we discovered those three were, how you say, ripping us off. So, it was only the brother from our business that cared, and he did what he did with his friend behind our backs. The reason for our continuing concern in you, is because not long after your arrest and release, many of our businesses have come of interest to the police and we believe that because of your grudge against us you have been spying again and giving them information. Are we correct?"

"No! Why would you think that? I live up here now and most of your business is down south. I just did what I needed to do. As much as I hate everything you do and represent, what would be the point of me continuing to disrupt you when I know that all that would happen is, even if your particular racket gets busted, a similar bunch of crooks will soon come along and take your place. It doesn't have to be someone snooping around and giving the police information it may just be that you lot are finally in their spotlight. And, about time too."

"We have means of knowing that the information is coming from someone who has a grudge against us."

"How can you possibly say that if you don't know who it is? I really don't understand why I'm your number one suspect, when there must be dozens who want to see you lot go down, especially some of your previous employees that you treat like dirt."

The boss sighed and said, "Let's just say we have girls who work for us and they are visited by all kinds of men from all walks of life. Many of them are professionals with high ranking jobs who can't resist joining our girls in the shower and leaving all kinds of information in their pockets for us to copy while they do. Or they leave their cars parked close by and their registration numbers can be very useful to us in the future. So, as I am telling you that we know there is definitely an informant you can guess what type of organisation our source works for, but unfortunately he is unable to obtain the identity due to security restrictions."

"Well it's not me, I assure you. Think about it, if it were, and I wanted to blow your business apart the best thing I could do to achieve that would be to take these two to the nearest police station with their weapons and phones. They would both go to prison for years. And, given the right incentive they might well implicate you and your business. That together with the interrogation of their phone histories could cause you an awful lot of trouble. But I don't want that. I just want a peaceful life from now on."

"You could do that, that's for sure, so perhaps it's not you causing our problems. One of the other names mentioned who could be doing this, as he blames us for the death of his sister, was someone who once worked for us who called himself Jorge. I'm sure to do what you did, you must have spent some time at the place where he and the others all worked, did you ever meet this Jorge?"

Dutch truthfully replied, "George, no I don't know anyone called George." At the same time wondering if Jorge, an illegal immigrant, who had assisted him in killing three of the cartel by setting their office on fire at the Lewes car wash site, was still managing to evade the immigration authorities. If so, was he still wreaking revenge on the cartel? If he were, Dutch hoped that Jorge, which was a false name, would be successful and remain lucky.

"Okay you have convinced me that you are not the person we are looking for. If you can let those two go I can assure you that we will not worry you anymore. What did he mean that you have an army there?"

"Let's just say that I have some good friends. I'm sure your two boys will tell you all about just how well equipped and organised we are, so if you do ever consider revisiting me, I suggest that you think again. What I propose to do now is to take these two monkeys and point them south towards the motorway. To show you that I have no intention of further disrupting your business I am giving them back their phones. But, I am keeping and destroying the more dangerous items as I would be stupid to give them back, as I am not going to have what they may be used for in the future on my conscience."

"They are not easy to get hold of these days, but I understand. Those two idiots will have to pay for them when they get back here, but they will be having more problems than that."

"So, we have a deal, I let these two go and your mob stay out of my life forever?"

"If what you say is true, then yes it's a deal."

"That's what I wanted to hear. Tell your two goons that and I will send them packing straight away."

Dutch increased the volume of the phone and held it so both men to hear their boss say, "It's over, just get back here straight away."

Dutch terminated the call, being fully aware that he couldn't wholly trust the word of a hardened gangster, but he felt that he had done all he could possibly do to have convinced him that he wasn't the person who was currently disrupting their operation. He was still reeling from the surprise that apparently the cartel had not been chasing him since he had killed five of their gang. It appeared from what was said that he had almost done them a favour by disposing of the two drunken sexual perverts responsible for raping Melanie, and the three killed in the fire, who were apparently embezzling the gang's cash. The explanation about the brother of one of the men that was killed in the fire, seeking personal revenge also made sense. If the gang did consider reneging on their pact, perhaps when the two failed assassins described the fire power that the group possessed it may well convince them to leave well enough alone. Then it suddenly dawned on him, he had unnecessarily uprooted his family and moved from one end of the country to another due to a threat that didn't even exist. His negative thoughts regarding the move were soon dispelled when he considered how happy they all were living there, and how it could only get better now if he could fully relax his guard. He still missed the South Downs but the Lakes and fells were more than an excellent substitute.

Dutch then placed the phone back into the bag and hailed Ross.

As Ross walked towards Dutch and the two captives, "He commented, Are we doing some digging then?"

"No, lucky for them I have come to an agreement with their boss and as there appears to be a misunderstanding they can go. But they can remain cuffed up until we get well away from here."

Dutch then ushered Ross aside and in a low voice so that the men could not hear, "What I would like to do now is to ship these two out of here but I will need some more help as I can't trust them even if it is sorted out with their boss. Have you got a couple of spare ski masks that we can fit back to front so they will never be able to find their way back here should they ever be stupid enough to try to return?"

"I'll get some from the store. They won't have a clue where they are. What with you having given them the run around, and no signs from that approach indicating what this place is. I can help with the transportation; how much help do you need?"

"Cheers mate, I really owe you and the lads for this. I thought if we get one of the group to drive the Beemer and you drive my wagon, with me sitting in the back keeping an eye on both Knob Head and Dick Head here. Then we can find a spot somewhere between Windermere and Kendal to kick them out and they can get on their way back to whatever punishment awaits them."

"I will get Jack to drive the Beemer as he was the one who shot the window out when he was told to just miss the bloody thing."

Dutch laughed out loud at his comment.

"What's so funny?"

"That so much reminded me of Michael Caine's famous comment from the movie The Italian Job, "You're only supposed to blow the bloody doors off!"

Ross then became aware of how he had accidentally mimicked the well-known film quote, and also found what he had said amusing.

Dutch then quipped, "I hope it's their bosses car then they will be even further in the shit. We better search that car, just in case when we let them loose they turn some other weapons on us."

"Good shout, I'll get Jack and we will take a look before we head off."

Dutch stood over the gang members in total silence as he now had no need or desire to speak with either man who only a short while ago had been willing to shoot him, leaving him for dead on a country road.

They had served any use that he had for them and now wanted the murderous scum bags out of the area as quickly as possible. He wished that circumstances were different so that he could hand them to the police. But, that would have aggravated the gang further and may also have brought police attention to his own past misdemeanours. He had to be satisfied with what appeared to be the end of the long torturous affair.

He was well aware that he was taking an enormous risk, but was hopeful that he had made the right deal.

Ross and Jack then completed the search of the BMW and informed Dutch that it only contained personal items and clothing apart from a small box of bullets, which Ross retained and placed in the game bag that still hung around Dutch's neck.

Once all were positioned in their respective transport, Dutch placed the turned ski masks over the gang members heads and checked that the hand restraints were still taught and incapacitating. He also reminded both that if they were to play up, rather than use the shotgun which would make a terrible mess of his bus, he was still in possession of their loaded pistols.

As planned, Ross drove the tour bus through minor roads, closely followed by Jack in the BMW. After a twenty-minute journey they stopped in a small wooded clearing at the side of the A591, where both gangsters were compliant as they were relieved of their masks and bindings. Once they were seated inside their vehicle, Dutch handed them the seized mobile phones, and, with his hand held menacingly in the game bag, despite their pleas refused to hand back their weapons. Once pointed in the direction of the M6 motorway the two disgruntled villains left.

The three bye standers couldn't help but jest about how uncomfortable their long journey would be with no rear window and the forecast of rain. Also, how they must be re-considering their agreement to return to an inevitable punishment, which at the very minimum they could expect would be a return to car washing duties.

On returning to the Airsoft site, all seven members of the group involved in the incident participated in a debriefing. They agreed that their actions in assisting with resolution of the situation, as exciting and dramatic as it had been, should remain just between themselves. Dutch's decision to protect Melanie's privacy and not to expand on the history of the event would be respected.

After departing from group Dutch thought about the valuable assistance that Ross and the others had afforded him. He realised that much of the threatening words that Ross had used were merely to intimidate their captives to make them to comply, and had no genuine intention of participating in any killing. He couldn't help but wonder that would Ross have handed him his shotgun, had he known that he had previously killed five members of the gang, and if given no other option was willing to dispose of two more, for him and his family to live in peace. Dutch would never know the answer to his own question, as he had no intention of ever revealing the full facts to Ross, no matter how much a friend he considered him to be.

Dutch informed Ross that he would take responsibility to dispose of the guns, ammunition, and knife, but was left with the dilemma as to how. His first thought was to safely conceal them until the next firearms amnesty, but on reading the official amnesty website he immediately rejected the notion, as there was a note of caution to the effect that if any forensic examination revealed that any surrendered firearm found to have been used in any criminal activity would give rise to further police investigation. Knowing where the weapons had originated from, Dutch had little doubt that either could have been used in serious crime, therefore preventing him from forfeiting them without possible repercussions. He was left with no other alternative to break the guns down and to scatter the pieces in some of the deepest lakes. He was disappointed in littering the lakes in this manner but found solace, as being all metal objects, they would soon disappear in the silt lake beds never to be found, or to be of further danger. Dutch had briefly considered that should the gang renege on their agreement it may have been advisable for him to stash one of the weapons and ammunition in safe location, in a similar way that he had hidden a war trophy pistol in the past, but it had been the availability of such a weapon that had contributed to his reckless behaviour which had resulted in years of turmoil for him and his family.

Later that afternoon following the disposal of the guns, Dutch entered the family home and was immediately met by a happy and carefree Melanie, who greeted him,

"Hi Dennis, how was your day?"

Even though he had survived an attempted assassination and possibly solved the precarious problem that had haunted them for years, he had no intention of dragging the matter up, because as far as Melanie knew they had left the worry behind when moving to the area. He had no wish to unsettle her new happy and confident self, so he merely replied:

"Not bad love, what's for tea?"

CHAPTER 10

Rat Trap *(1978)*

Artists: Boomtown Rats
Writer: Bob Geldof

As a token of appreciation to Ross and the fellow members of the group who assisted him in the very precarious situation Dutch treated them all to a meal at a local Indian restaurant, where very little was discussed with regard to the incident but if anything was referred to, it was heavily censored with winks and whispers.

To further demonstrate his gratitude to the group he fully immersed himself in many of the local problems bought to their attention by making himself available as often as his commitments would allow.

During the year following the foiled assassination attempt Dutch was fully involved in three particularly interesting and successful tasks, which disrupted criminal activity, not only in the town but also in the smaller nearby villages.

Most towns and villages house a 'Jack the Lad' or 'Del Boy' type character, equivalent to the second world war Spiv, who could obtain a pair of nylon stockings or fresh meat when all other legitimate sources had none. To make a profit such characters would obtain their desired merchandise by methods both fair, but mainly foul. Those who chose to take the criminal route were popularly known as receivers or fences and were not only a vital source, useful to both thieves and burglars to pass on their illicit gains, but also popular with some members of the general community seeking a bargain, with little concern as to how or where the property had been obtained.

A particular suspected 'receiver' Jackson, nicknamed Bonzo who lived in a village in the south Lake District had been suspected by the police for 'fencing' stolen goods for a considerable time, but despite carrying out search warrants at his address and grounds, nothing incriminating had ever been found. Jackson was a fearsome and intimidating character that ensured that very few would ever inform the police regarding his clandestine business.

The matter had been bought to the attention of the group following one of Jackson's long-term neighbours overhearing a reference to Jackson whilst frequenting the village pub. The neighbour had unwittingly informed a member of the group that he had overheard a conversation between two known criminal associates of Jackson referring to him as Bonzo 'three sheds'. The source of the information who lived in the same terraced block of housing as Jackson had thought it odd as he could plainly see, and knew that Jackson's rear garden had only ever accommodated two sheds.

The group member concerned feigned any interest in the information, but at his first opportunity informed Ross, who arranged discreet observations on Jackson's address. The observations were coordinated from an old, inconspicuous van belonging to one of the group, which was parked in a nearby street, in such a position that it gave a clear view of both the front and rear gates of Jackson's address. As at least three members were required for the venture, it meant that the observations were infrequent and the few that had been carried out had proved fruitless. However, on one occasion Jackson was followed to a block of garages which excited the observers, but when he removed his car it was established that very little property of any significance was contained inside.

Despite the disappointment, as the van was soon to be sold as the owner had no current use for the vehicle, the observations continued whenever manpower was available. During one evening of observations, Dutch, with his task partner Mark, a financial risk manager, who, as a former insurance fraud investigator was vastly experienced in surveillance techniques were sitting together on a bench in a nearby park, and to divert any suspicion were accompanied by Jodie, when they received a message from the observer in the van that Jackson was on the move on foot. Having received a description of the man and his clothing, Dutch and Mark were directed to a narrow woodland pathway that ran adjacent to the rear of Jackson's home. After walking only, a short distance, the path took a sharp left-hand bend where they were confronted by a closed sturdy metal gate and wire fencing. A number of signs attached to the fencing indicated that beyond the gate was a council-controlled allotment. As the heavy-duty cable combination lock around the gate was not secured to the fence post they entered the grounds. They slowly emerged from the tree-lined path into the wide expanse of the open allotment, with Dutch carefully restraining Jodie close to his side by the use of a lead.

As it was late evening and light was beginning to fade there was understandably no sign of any persons working amongst the many well-maintained garden plots. Suddenly Mark gave Dutch an urgent nudge with his elbow, followed by tugging on his sleeve, gently pulling him back into the darkness of the tree-covered pathway. Mark then pointed towards a small wooden shed tucked in the corner of the allotment. The door of the shed was partially open and a flicker of light could be seen inside. With both men realising what they had possibly discovered they jubilantly exchanged a thumbs up gesture. Keen not to be seen, they both took note of the precise location of the shed, at the same time observing that it had no window and looked particularly solid compared to most of the many other older, flimsier sheds scattered about. They further noticed that the plot on which the shed stood was one of the very few that contained far more weeds than fruit or vegetables. Before leaving their position they were able to confirm that the person in the shed was wearing the bright coloured anorak as had been described to them.

Both then left the allotment and once clear of the area made a hurried call reporting what they had seen to the occupant of the van. During the conversation, the observer informed Dutch and Mark that, at that precise moment, he was in the process of watching Jackson emerge from the path and returning to his home. Jackson was holding a small item in a plastic bag, which he had not been carrying on his outward journey.

All three elated men then met together when it was decided that the spotter would make the anonymous call to Kendal police station regarding their suspicions.

A week later the news of Jackson's arrest was comprehensibly reported in the West Moorland Gazette, describing that a search warrant had been executed at a village allotment and suspected stolen property had been found in a small shed within the grounds. The article further stated that a local thirty-five-year-old man had been arrested and bailed, pending further enquiries regarding the recovered property. A police source was quoted as saying that the shed had been extremely secure and was protected by a simple silent alarm system, which could be monitored from a nearby dwelling.

A series of thefts from unattended vehicles which had occurred over a long period came to the attention the alliance. Some of which occurred at beauty spots during daylight hours and others during darkness in the busier streets of the district. Early in the series of thefts the police had placed a trap car in the vicinity of previous crimes. The car was subsequently broken into, which resulted in the thief being automatically locked inside and a silent alarm triggered, sending a coded signal to police officer's personal radios. Before a police patrol could reach the scene the thief had kicked out the rear window of the car and made good his or her escape. From methods used by the offender police believed that the same person was responsible for all, or most of the thefts, and from evidence found believed the person to be a drug user.

The details of the thefts were widely published within the district, advising car owners to secure their vehicles whilst unattended, and not to leave anything of value on display inside.

Following the escape from the trap car there was a short interval before identical thefts reoccurred. It was at this point that the group decided that when volunteers were available they would make some casual night-time observations in the most vulnerable locations.

Over a period of a fortnight the group had managed to cover most nights, and during one night when Dutch was engaged in trying to locate the thief a car had been broken into.

Dutch took this personally and made himself available for further periods. Once again using Melanie's small inconspicuous Fiat and partnered by Jo, who was herself an ex-soldier, so the couple had plenty to discuss as they sat waiting and observing from the darkest corners of a number of streets that they considered would be most favourable to the thief.

As both had work commitments they decided to conclude the task at 3am, which would then give them time to grab a few hours' sleep. With no sightings, once again a disappointed Dutch commenced to drive to where Jo had parked her own car. As he drove along a dark street the full beam emitted from the Fiat's headlights illuminated a line of parked cars on the offside of the road.

As the lights shone through the rear window of an old silver Vauxhall, Dutch could clearly see a person sitting in the driver's seat. Dutch initially thought that it was possibly a person having just parked or just about to drive off, but as they got closer to the Vauxhall he saw the figure slowly slide down the seat and out of his sight. Dutch instinctively knew by the person's suspicious movement that the intention was to hide from view, and so not wishing to spook the occupant, he slowly brought the Fiat to a halt and reversed into a space between two parked vehicles. Whilst carrying out the manoeuvre he continued to watch the car, at the same time informing Jo what he had seen. Once stationary, Dutch turned off the Fiat's lights, grabbed his torch, at the same time instructing Jo to casually approach the vehicle and to ready herself for any attempt from the occupant to exit from the nearside door. As Dutch left his car he could see that the occupant lowered from sight had still not emerged into a normal sitting position. On reaching the driver's door of the two-door car, Dutch shone his torch inside and could see a slim figure in dark clothing remaining in the driver's seat but bent fully forwards with head down towards the floor. Dutch tapped on the window and directed his voice towards the occupant,

"Excuse me, is this your car?"

The person inside did not move and his question went unanswered.

"If it is yours, why are you hiding and not answering me?"

Again, there was no response from the person inside.

Now certain that the occupant had something to conceal, Dutch attempted to open the door but it was locked, and he could see that the door lock button next to the window had been depressed. After Jo had confirmed that the passenger door was also locked, Dutch forcibly tapped on the window and in a stern voice loudly said, "You can't sit in that position forever and we aren't going away until you give me some explanation as to what you are playing at."

Following his remarks, a gaunt, pale youth aged about eighteen years of age sat fully up into the seat and replied, "I'm just trying to sleep. I've got nowhere else to go."

"Who does this car belong to?"

"I don't know, it was open."

Dutch then shone his torch at the passenger side of the dashboard and saw that the glove compartment was fully open and empty, but what appeared to have been inside was now spread over the passenger seat, causing Dutch to remark, "You're telling me that you are only sleeping in there but I'll bet the owner of this car didn't leave that stuff all over the seat. You were looking for something to nick weren't you?"

"There's nothing in here worth nicking, so you can let me go."

"Not a chance mate. You wait there. Keep an eye on that door Jo."

Jo, who was standing beside the passenger door acknowledged his suggestion and lent her body against the door preventing the possible escape route.

Just as Dutch was contemplating his next course of action he heard the noise of the opening of an upstairs window from a terraced house behind him. Still standing against the driver's door he turned his head and saw a black male leaning out of the open window who angrily pronounced,

"What the fuck are you doing next to my car?"

Dutch replied, "That's handy, we needed to find the owner as you've got an unwelcome guest inside."

"What do you mean?"

Dutch pointing to the youth sitting in the driver's seat, "We were just passing when we saw this bloke trying to hide inside."

"Cheeky bastard. Hang on I'll be straight down."

A short time later the man appeared from the house followed by a younger man, who was introduced as the car owner's son.

After Dutch had explained exactly what he had seen, the owner then noticed his property spread across the seat and became extremely annoyed and threatened to drag the youth out of the car. Dutch managed to calm him down and suggested that it would be foolish for him to assault the youth and get into trouble, when the best option was to prevent any assault allegations, and give the intruder no chance of escape by leaving him imprisoned inside the vehicle until the arrival of the police. As the owners son telephoned for police attendance, Dutch together with the owner examined the doors and windows but could not find any damage. They asked the person inside how he had entered but he continued to hang his head and gave no reply.

The owner showed Dutch his ignition key for the car but admitted that he may have forgotten to lock it as he never left anything of value inside.

With neither Jo, nor he wishing to provide witness statements to the police Dutch said to the owner:

"Look, neither me or my lady friend can afford to get officially involved here. Both of our respective partners think that we are with other people somewhere else, so we can't hang around any longer. It will make no difference as he's got no excuse for being in your car and rifling through the contents. You do understand the difficult position we are in don't you?"

As soon as the words had passed his lips he looked across the roof of the car at Jo who looked astounded at his comment.

The car owner laughed and responded, "Mate, I've been there, done it, and got the Tee shirt. You both get going, and don't worry I've calmed down now, I ain't going to whack him as he looks like a right scrawny junkie who might just snuff it if I did."

Having shaken hands with the man, Dutch together with Jo entered the Fiat, and to prevent any details of his car being recorded, Dutch turned the car around and drove off for a short distance before switching on his lights.

As shocked as Jo was at what Dutch had said about their apparent illicit relationship, she found it quite amusing and congratulated Dutch on his quick thinking.

It was pleasing for Dutch, Jo, and the group as a whole when they later learnt that the thief had admitted attempted theft from the Vauxhall and had owned up to many of the previous reported thefts, which had been taken into consideration when sentenced to a term of imprisonment, incorporating a drugs rehabilitation programme.

Yet, one of Dutch's most satisfying assignments was not one involving the group, but one that he came across by chance.

Whilst browsing in the delicatessen counter in Sugdens' supermarket Dutch was approached by the manager Tony, with whom he had become very well acquainted since the incident involving the bread thefts.

After exchanging the usual pleasantries, Tony asked Dutch if he had heard about the recent mugging of a milkman on the outskirts of the town. Such offences were rare in the area, so news of such a crime travelled very quickly and Dutch was able to confirm that he was aware of the incident.

Tony then followed on his question by saying," According to Police appeals one of the two youths responsible was wearing a light blue sweatshirt with the word 'Physique' emblazoned on the chest."

"I didn't know that, but carry on."

"Well on Friday, the day before it happened, I was standing at the front of the shop looking onto the parade when I saw a teenager walking by angrily tearing up what I thought was a piece of paper and allowing the pieces to drop all over the pavement. I was enraged about it, because my shop gets the majority of the blame for the litter that is left around here.

"Without thinking about the possible consequences, I ran onto the parade and called out for him to come back and pick up his rubbish.

"To be honest, I expected him to give me a mouthful of abuse and walk off, but to my surprise he turned around and walked back to me. He was a tall athletic looking lad with an angry expression on his face and I anticipated an altercation, but after I told him that he was out of order as my shop was constantly under scrutiny from the local authority regarding the littering of paper, cans, and cartons, he became calm and apologised. He then started to pick up the pieces that he had thrown and I could see that they were of a photograph. As he collected them up he explained that he and a friend were up here on a camping holiday and that he had just received a text message from his long-term girlfriend who he had left behind informing him in no uncertain terms that she was finishing their relationship for good. His immediate reaction was to tear up her photograph and throw it away in anger."

"Job done then Tony, but you are now thinking he may be one of the muggers?"

"Maybe, because he was wearing an identical sweatshirt as described by the police. I know that brand is very popular at the moment as I have seen a few others about."

"It could well be him as I can't see any of the local lads mugging a milkman who could see them out and about at any time. What did he do with the pieces of the photograph?"

Tony, pointing to the pavement outside the shop responded, "He put them in that bin."

"Do you know when it was last emptied?"

Tony walked to the front window, "It looks full, I guess that it hasn't been emptied since then."

Following Dutch's suggestion that they should find something that they could tip the contents of the bin onto, Tony returned from the storeroom with a large piece of clear plastic sheeting and two pairs of plastic gloves.

Both then emptied the bin onto the sheeting and located each piece of torn photograph, which when pieced together showed the head and shoulders image of a young male and female. Tony identified the male as being the person who had torn up the photo. After returning the remainder of the litter into the bin the two men returned to Tony's office where the police were informed of their findings.

On the next occasion that Dutch visited the shop Tony told him that the police had taken copies of the recovered photograph to various local camp sites and the youth was traced. The 'Physique' sweatshirt was found hidden inside his sleeping bag. Both he and his friend were arrested and both had been identified by the milkman as being the attackers. Dutch enjoyed telling the unusual and fortuitous tale at the next group meeting.

CHAPTER 11

A Soldier's Memoir
(PTSD song 2013)

Artists: Joe Bachman
Writers: Joe Bachman, Mitch Rossell

Dutch had always been eternally grateful that despite experiencing numerous challenging and horrendous experiences, he had never, unlike some of his former colleagues had any serious psychological problems. Two of his closest friends and ex colleagues, David Crook nicknamed 'Davy' Crocket and James 'Dickie' Bird had been diagnosed, and were still suffering from PTSD (Post Traumatic Stress Disorder) following being caught up in an ambush during a tour of Iraq, which had resulted in a number of deaths in addition to life changing injuries to his two friends.

It had saddened him deeply to see the effect that the condition could cause to once fit, strong, and healthy men, and thought himself lucky not to have succumbed to the condition, as so many had. He often wondered why it affected some at varying degrees, but not others, such as himself, who despite also being seriously injured and involved in identical situations, could live with such horrors. Could it be that his tragic and unfortunate early life had prepared him for the shit storm that was to come?

Since his retirement from the army the only minor problems that he had encountered, that he thought may be connected to his former career, were reoccurring night sweats, which he considered were more likely to be caused by his excessive running. But, he always automatically ducked his head when hearing a loud bang, such as the noise from the exhaust of a misfiring motor engine, or being surprised by loud exploding fireworks.

To protect himself from negative thoughts Dutch tried not to mull over the more upsetting occurrences that he and colleagues had endured. However, this was to change, oddly triggered by some offensive comments directed towards him.

Dutch took an interest in some of the Military internet forums, and if a particular subject gained his interest he would occasionally make a comment or give his opinion was to cause him concern. It was not so much about the criticism on his written opinion, but what he considered to be an unprovoked and personal attack on himself.

The response to his contribution on a page discussing snipers tactics was titled 'Utter Garbage' and then continued to vehemently discredit Dutch's comments, without giving an alternative view on the subject. It further described Dutch's opinion as unbelievable, and as if written by a child. Also stating that he was ashamed to have once worked with the author of the piece, and was signed Vic J Palmer.

Dutch was forced to read it twice before he could believe that most of the vicious comments were directed at him personally and not towards the subject matter. The only Vic

Palmer he knew from his army days was a soldier of that name whom he did not know particularly well as he was a member of a different unit, and they had never worked closely together. He had never had a cross word with Palmer and Dutch knew that he was never a qualified sniper, so suspected that whoever had written the hurtful comments had used Palmer's name to discredit him to hide the writer's true identity. It was a mystery to Dutch as he could not understand why anybody would want to attack him in this way.

Dutch was so incensed by the insults that he took a screen shot of the remarks and electronically reported the matter to the site editor, who removed the comments immediately.

Despite the omission Dutch was so disgruntled at what he considered was unwarranted personal criticism that he decided to investigate who disliked him enough to respond with such disparaging remarks.

His search on social media sites soon revealed an ex-serviceman of the same name as the author of the remarks, as being a proprietor of a business in another part of the country.

A photograph on the business site identified the owner as being the former army serviceman, Palmer.

Dutch called the number given, which was answered:

"Vic Palmer speaking. How may I help?"

"Hello Vic, I'm not sure if you remember me, Dennis Dutch French?"

The introduction prompted a pensive reply, "Yes Dennis, I remember you."

"Vic, I'm just checking something out. Someone has made some particularly nasty comments about me on a website forum and attributed them to a Vic Palmer who apparently worked with me. That wasn't you was it Vic?"

The question was greeted by a few seconds silence followed by: "Yes it was me."

"What! Why would you do that? They weren't normal comments or criticisms, it was a personal character assassination."

"Because the article was absolute garbage. I have seen another piece that you have written and I didn't think much of that either, but this was even worse."

"That's fair enough, anyone is entitled to disagree with my opinion, but why refer to my writing as childish and unbelievable, making comments about something that you have no knowledge. You were never a sniper, were you?"

"No, but I can still have an opinion."

Of course, that is what a forum is all about, but that still doesn't make sense as to why you made snide remarks about me. Perhaps I should put some personal comments on your business website?"

"I will just remove them."

"Apart from you, everyone else on that forum agreed with my observations, and you have no expertise on the subject whatsoever."

"Did they really agree, or were they just thinking, poor old Dennis, let's just go with him?"

"I don't know what your problem with me is Vic, but if you carry on with this I will get very angry, as you are giving me no valid reason for your bad feelings towards me. I suspect that that there is more to this, than just an article on a forum."

"Okay, one of the reasons is that I didn't like the way you de-friended me and others on an ex services website."

"Well, that's a pathetic reason. I left that site together with others as some of the comments were getting far too personal over a political issue. Those of us who pulled out didn't like the way things were going, especially when it deteriorated into name calling, and if I remember correctly you were one of the instigators of such remarks. You seem to be getting very bitter and twisted in your old age. I'm warning you Vic drop it."

Following Dutch's comment, the line went dead.

Dutch was still fuming at what he considered was a pathetic reason for insulting him and immediately redialled the number but the call was not answered.

Both annoyed and confused, he then called his good friend and ex colleague Jon Shipway, who had also been his boss following his retirement from the army. Jon was one of the very few people that he had trusted with the knowledge of his present whereabouts.

The call was answered, "What sort of shit are you in this time Dutch?"

"Don't be like that mate I'm not always in trouble."

No that's true, only ninety-nine point nine per cent of each time you contact me."

"Well you will be pleased to know my troubles with that gang could be over."

"Why's that, have you finally disposed of the whole fucking lot of them?"

"Not quite, but it was all very amicable in the end."

"Thank Christ for that, so I finally don't have to panic each time you call. So, what do I owe the pleasure?"

"Don't be like that mate, you make me sound like a nuisance."

"If the cap fits wear it!"

"Why I am calling today is purely social with a simple question. Do you remember Vic Palmer?"

"Yeah vaguely, why, what's he been up to?"

"Insulting me for some reason or other."

"Jon interrupted, Well that doesn't make him a bad bloke."

That's the sort of response I expected from you! But I know that you don't really mean it, or I hope not anyway?"

"Got to have some banter mate, carry on."

"Well, I put what I thought was some constructive comments on a forum and he responded with some very personal remarks about me. Why I don't know…."

Jon interrupted, "Stop there. You are not the first person that I have heard complaining about comments he has made about others on various sites. He appears to have a few issues. So much so he has earned the nickname of 'Palmer the Charmer'."

"Do you know why he's so bitter then?"

"I understand from some of our former colleagues that he went out with some stress problems and it doesn't appear that things have improved over the years. It's been suggested that his aggression and irritability could possibly be symptoms of PTSD, so don't take it personally. It's just that you raised your head above the parapet with your post and were there to be shot at."

Dutch laughingly responded: "That's ironic as the entire post was references to snipers. Oh well, that accounts for it. So, he hasn't particularly targeted me, he appears to have a problem with anyone and everyone. Now I know that I can let the matter rest and hope that he gets help and sorts himself out, otherwise he's going to make a lot of enemies with those who don't know of his condition."

"There's that saying, you can take the soldier out of the war, but you can't take the war out of the soldier, which may well apply to him."

"Both him, and many others I'm afraid."

"Yes, and there by the grace of God go us. I thought that you were calling to invite us up for that holiday you promised."

"Anytime now mate. I wasn't going to let you and Sal up here while that gang were still after me."

The conversation then continued with general leg pulling between the two close friends.

That night whilst laying in bed Dutch couldn't help continuing to think about all the victims of PTSD, not only soldiers from UK forces but also those in the States who had also served in the same war zones of Iraq and Afghanistan. The suicide rate amongst war veterans and serving soldiers from both countries suffering from the condition was alarmingly high.

The initial event and the following conversations of that day prevented him from getting a wink of sleep, as his thoughts were not only with Crocket and Palmer but with all serviceman suffering from serious stress-related problems.

As he lay awake, he considered how fortunate he had been to be unaffected by any serious psychological problems. Although he was aware that although symptoms of PTSD usually occurred within days, weeks, or months after a traumatic event, there had been instances where it had gripped some after a decade or more.

His thoughts then turned to some of the life threatening and harrowing moments that he had experienced, of which there were many.

His first recollection of being seriously distressed was when as an infant he inadvertently learnt of the circumstances surrounding the deaths of his parents. Having eventually come to terms with the horrors, due to his tender years and never having met his father, and only being able to vaguely remember his mother, his caring grandparents proved to be more than suitable substitutes. But, the stigma of being orphaned and knowing of his parents' demise remained with him throughout his adolescence.

At a very young age, whilst fleeing from a group of older bullying kids, he had run into the road and was hit by a car. Miraculously, he only suffered cuts and bruises and whilst tending to his injuries his widely celebrated mystic grandmother Connie, told him that he had lost the first of the nine lives that he had been allocated. Although confused by the remark at the time, he was to be reminded of the comment on many occasions throughout the years to come.

Shortly after joining the parachute regiment his unit was deployed to the conflict in Northern Ireland. Dutch at seventeen was deemed too young to go on the tour but eighteen-year-old Derek Bowman, only a few weeks older than Dutch, was selected. Dutch was extremely disappointed in not being included, but this was to change when the alternative assignment that he was given gave him the opportunity to meet and form a relationship with Melanie. During his absence from his unit Dutch received the news that Derek had been shot and killed at a checkpoint in Belfast. Whilst being very saddened by the news Dutch couldn't help but consider that if he had been able to join his unit as he had wished, it could have well been him at that checkpoint.

He considered that his third close shave to death occurred on a lads' night out in a nightclub. A group of local men identified Dutch and his colleagues as soldiers and goaded them throughout the evening. The continual insults developed into a fight and as the small group of soldiers were heavily outnumbered by the mob they were soon split up. Dutch found himself up against a man brandishing a knife and was stabbed in the neck. During his hospitalisation he was informed by doctors that although he had lost a lot of blood he had been extremely lucky as the knife had partially cut his carotid artery. If it had severed it completely he would not have survived.

Dutch considered that he would have avoided being stabbed if his reactions had not been affected by drink and from that moment on he hardly ever drank alcohol again.

Whilst serving in the Middle East Dutch was part of a forward party of soldiers waiting for clearance to proceed to a forward position when a small motorcycle approached the unit. The rider of the machine was signalled to stop but instead accelerated towards the soldiers who opened fire, hitting the rider, but not before he was able to steer the machine into an armoured troop carrier, instantly killing himself. When they examined the traditionally robed man they saw an electronic triggering device attached to his wrist. They were later to discover from the bomb disposal unit that the rucksack on the deceased's back contained an explosive and hundreds of large nails. Had the triggering device not been shaken loose by the motorcycle's bumpy journey on the rough roads there would have been many serious casualties.

By far the most serious injuries that he had sustained during combat was in a night-time operation in Afghanistan, when he was required to blow open a large metal door and grill to allow accompanying soldiers to enter in the hope of releasing hostages held by Taliban fighters. Whilst setting the explosive, a fuse proved to be detective and failed, forcing Dutch to use an improvised firing method, knowing that once primed he would have little time to get clear of the blast. With the success or failure of the operation in his hands, he felt that he had no choice but to proceed despite the grave personal risk. Having triggered the explosive, he ran for the nearest cover of a low wall, but before he reached it the device exploded and he was struck in the back by flying shrapnel, causing him to be hospitalised for several weeks. Despite the setback, the operation was a complete success and for his gallant efforts Dutch was awarded the Military Cross. The huge scars that remained on his back was a testament to his bravery and a constant reminder of the mission.

Of all things, it happened to be a small piece of woven material that not only saved his life, but also others. Once again whilst in the middle East, as part of a forward foot patrol approaching a small village recently abandoned by

Islamic state fighters, Dutch felt that his boot was loose on his foot. Whilst crouching down to retie his lace he remained vigilant, and as he looked towards a parked battered truck he noticed a suspicious device resting on the top of a rear wheel, partly concealed by the wheel arch. He immediately halted the advance party and bomb disposal officers were dispatched to the scene. The device was found to be a large IED, which, if detonated, would have wiped out many of the soldiers present. There was no doubt that if he had not stooped down when he did the device would have gone unnoticed. For that reason, that same shoelace, which holds his dog tag, still hangs around his neck today.

Whilst in Norway on a joint military training exercise, he was with other troops crossing a temporary pontoon over a fast-flowing river, when the structure was unexpectantly struck by an ice pack. Many of the troops, wearing heavy winter clothing and all carrying heavy back packs, were thrown into the icy cold water. The weight of their soaked clothing and baggage, together with the freezing water made it extremely difficult for all of the jettisoned soldiers to keep their heads above water. Fortunately for Dutch the force of the current pushed him towards the riverbank and a fallen pine tree. Dutch was able to grab a branch and hold on until help arrived. As he was removed from his wooden liberator suffering from hyperthermia he requested that one of his rescuers snap a twig from the tree. The sprig still remains in his service memorabilia box as a memory of yet another lucky escape. Two other soldiers on the bridge had not been afforded the same luck, and had drowned.

Many years passed until he considered that he had cheated death once more. The event occurred during his forced departure to Venezuela when working as a bodyguard, an attempt was made to kidnap his oil executive boss. Shots fired from a very powerful rifle missed his head by inches, an incident which subsequently caused his return to the UK.

Dutch had calculated that this had been his eighth lost life and if his grandmother's prophecy was correct he had only one left in the bank. But, he was unaware that a very damaging piece of CCTV footage had been inadvertently destroyed which would have convicted him of killing the two men responsible for raping his wife. Such evidence would have undoubtably resulted in him receiving life imprisonment. His grandmother would have considered the implications of such a sentence as a further lost life, therefore, the loss of his ninth life made him a mere mortal.

At the conclusion of his thoughts, just as most of the world were waking, he was now feeling ready to sleep. But, before attempting to do so he considered that, despite all that had happened to him, his only psychological problems were over his immense dislike for bullies and snide individuals who professed to be colleagues, but could at any time stab someone in the back to suit their own agenda.

Because of all of the occasions when he could have and should have died, every morning as soon as he awoke and opened his eyes to the world he would say a quiet thank you to whoever or whatever it was allowing him to continue to walk the planet. He firmly believed that despite him cheating death on numerous occasions someone whether it be God, his parents or Connie were in some way instrumental in his continual survival.

CHAPTER 12

Seen the Light *(2003)*

Artists: Supergrass
Writers: Supergrass

During his lifetime, of all of the hair-raising moments and near-death experiences, the one that Dutch looked back on as being the most satisfying was not one where his life had been in danger, but where others had been in peril.

It was on his second tour of Iraq, and he had long been a trained sniper, but apart from regular marksman training had not been operationally involved in the role for some time.

All was to change, when Dutch, resting in a shady area inside camp between escort duties was urgently summonsed to the camp command post. There he was told that a sniper was required immediately, and asked if there any reason that he was unable to fulfil the task. Dutch jumped at the opportunity as it was a role to which he had been longing to return.

He soon mentally prepared himself for the mission, which was to assist in the extraction of troops from a FV432 armoured personnel carrier that had struck a large IED which had incapacitated the vehicle. The occupants of the vehicle were under fire from whom they believed was a lone sniper positioned on the eastern side of the valley, who had wounded one of the crew, who had left the vehicle to inspect the damage caused by the explosion.

Despite his injury the soldier had managed to re-enter the carrier and his wound was not considered life threatening but in need of prompt medical attention.

Dutch was then shown maps and aerial photographs of the Wadi (Arabic word for valley, ravine, or channel that is dry except in the rainy season) and its surrounding sand and rocky slopes in which the carrier was marooned.

He carefully inspected his immaculately maintained L96 AI 7.62 calibre rifle, and mentally ticked off all that he would need for the proposed mission. He equipped himself with a chest rig so everything he required would be at hand, thereby minimising his movements. Despite the threat of IED's, Dutch chose not to wear body armour, as he considered it may compromise his shooting ability.

He was asked if he required the aid of a spotter, but he declined the offer as he preferred to work alone in such a situation and felt confident to do so with the aid of his personal rangefinder device. Dutch felt that with such little cover available a person moving alone was less likely to be seen by the opposition forces.

Once fully camouflaged in a ghillie suit and helmet, and having tested his radio, he plotted his most advantageous position and was then transported to a point where it was thought to be far enough away to be undetected from within the Wadi.

While carrying his sniper rifle in a valise strapped across his back, and with both hands firmly gripped on a his SA80 assault rifle should he need to defend himself at short range, Dutch cautiously stalked his way towards the edge of the valley. At the earliest opportunity he sat down behind a large mound and again studied his map to confirm his location by compass. He also noted the position of the sun. Before moving on he took a large gulp of water from his canteen as he was aware his movements would soon have to be severely restricted.

As he approached the sparse vegetation surrounding the summit of the Wadi he crawled the last few yards and lay prone behind the thickest of the surprisingly green bushes. He then slowly and methodically parted the tall grass and thin branches that were obstructing his view into the valley. With the sun directly behind him he confidently employed his binoculars to scour the scene below. He immediately noticed the serious damage to the wheels and track at the front of the personnel carrier, which was positioned at an angle across the rocky path, which during heavy rain, was a riverbed as water ran through the ravine. As he closely inspected the vehicle he could see a dark patch on the rocky surface below the rear door, as the damage caused by the explosion was at the front of the vehicle Dutch presumed that the stain was caused from the blood of the wounded soldier. He then turned the binoculars towards the more obvious points from where the shot may have emanated.

Dutch then deployed his radio and attempted to make contact by calling the call sign of the damaged vehicle.

"Hello Whiskey 22 Alpha, this is 61 Charlie, radio check over."

After a short while his transmission was answered, "61 Charlie this is Wiskey22 Alpha, you are ok to me."

Having established good and readable radio commu-
nication, Dutch requested that the occupants provide him
with a rough idea of from where they believed the shot had
been fired. The crew replied that they had deduced that
from the position of their vehicle and the point where their
injured colleague had been when struck, the single bullet
had been fired from a position high on the north eastern
side of the valley.

Having established that the injured crew member had
been shot in the right shoulder as he exited the rear offside
opening door, Dutch was in agreement with their assessment.
He was also able to establish that they had stemmed the blood
flow from the soldier's wound and that he was comfortable,
having been administered a painkiller.

There was no guarantee that the sniper had remained
in the same position, but due to limited options of hides,
Dutch felt that there was a good chance that the sniper had
not moved as he obviously had an ideal position to prevent
the occupants of the carrier leaving the vehicle, under fear
of being shot.

Like most soldiers previously deployed in Iraq and
Afghanistan, Dutch knew that it was regular Taliban, Al
Qaeda, and ISIS tactics to set up a number of hidden booby
trap devices and leave a lone sniper nearby to pick off any
survivors from the resulting explosion. If this particular sniper
were still present he would also be vigilantly watching and
waiting for the inevitable arrival of assistance to extract the
stranded personnel, when they, too, would become his prey.

Although Dutch had been deployed in the role of sniper
in the past, he had never been involved in sniper versus

sniper before, so he hoped his adversary was still present. He felt sure that his opposition was not the renown Juba, the pseudonym for the crack ISIS sniper with the reputation of having killed 37 soldiers. Dutch felt sure that such a marksman would not have merely wounded such an easy target as the soldier leaving the personnel carrier.

Dutch then used his binoculars to closely study the area that he considered the sniper would possibly favour for his hide. Amongst the most likely sites were those in a similar position to his behind the undergrowth on the edge of the Wadi. There were also further scattered thickets and two small derelict stone-built shepherds' huts at different heights on the steep slopes.

Having made his observations, Dutch again contacted the crew of the stranded carrier and requested someone to open the rear door slowly and carefully, as if someone were about to attempt an exit. He instructed them to give him five minutes to prepare, and to keep well clear of the opening and to leave it ajar until he instructed them to close it.

Dutch then moved his body to the most comfortable prone position for firing, replaced his helmet with a baseball cap, then pulled the ghillie suit hood over the cap, a more suitable head covering, keeping any camouflage out of his face, and giving eye relief from the bright surroundings. Having done so, he made a quick visual check of his rifle, and before loading the magazine, shook it to stimulate all the propellent inside the case for a more accurate shot. After adjusting the telescopic sight, he watched for the door to open. As soon as it moved he turned his attention to the other side of the valley. By looking through the magnified site he slowly examined the possible positions that he had identified. As he scanned each one, he saw a glint of light emanating from a hole in the lower part of a stone wall which was once part of a shepherd's hut.

Dutch increased the magnification on his sight and peered into the small hole from where a rock had been removed from the centre of a lower row of the damaged stone structure. On close examination he could clearly see the tip of a rifle barrel protruding from the hole, and in the blackness of the shadow within the void the weapon's telescopic sight glass lens was reflecting the penetrating sunlight. The gunman had clearly taken the bait and would be homing in his sight, eagerly anticipating a soldier emerging from the open door of the carrier. Dutch quickly used his rangefinder which calculated that the distance between him and the wall was a little under 600 metres. He further evaluated the prevailing strength and direction of the wind and the differential of height between his position and that of the sniper. Once his formula was complete he adjusted the dials on the scope with the necessary number of 'clicks', and took careful aim at the void. Although he could not see any part of his adversary behind the wall, he could envisage exactly where he was in relation to the position of the protruding weapon and its scope. Dutch was confident that as long as his shot was accurate, even if the bullet didn't prove immediately fatal he would definitely incapacitate the sniper by wounding him in the head.

Dutch raised his weapon and once he felt comfortable and relaxed, reverted into his controlled breathing routine and whilst doing so stared down his scope until the cross hairs were fully focused on the dark void from where the sniper's rifle was protruding. As soon as the hairs were situated where he considered the sniper's head to be, he took a deep breath, then paused the exhalation and slowly started to apply gentle, continuous pressure on the trigger, once satisfied he released the shot and then exhaled fully, at the same time re-cocking his rifle, should he have missed his target and needed to re-engage.

He immediately knew that his shot had been accurate when he saw the protruding barrel suddenly raise and point upwards in a manner as if it was no longer supported by the rifleman. Dutch considered that no self-respecting sniper would leave his rifle in such an exposed position, unless dead or severely injured.

He waited a few minutes to observe any further movement, and, when there was none, he informed the carrier crew of his possible success, but instructed them to remain inside the vehicle until a rescue plan had been decided. Dutch then contacted the waiting release team who would need to sweep for further explosive devices before recovering the troops and the damaged vehicle. Whilst this operation was taking place Dutch continued to observe the wall and surrounding area in case the sniper's rifle was moved or there were further insurgents nearby.

Following the discovery and deactivation of two further concealed IED's, the immediate area of the path was given the all clear, and those in the carrier were able to leave the vehicle, enabling the injured soldier to be removed to the field hospital. Under the guidance of Dutch from his elevated position, a unit then moved cautiously forwards towards the sniper's hide. After reaching the wall and declaring the site safe they requested Dutch to join them. Before leaving his position Dutch located the single discharged shell case that had held the fatal bullet, and secured it in his pocket.

As Dutch stood over the prone dead body of the sniper he saw that his shot through the 'loop hole' had penetrated the right temple, just below his victim's black bandana, exactly the spot he believed he was aiming at in the darkness behind the wall. Dutch momentarily pondered as to why his opposition had made such an elementary mistake as to aim his telescopic sight of the Dragunov rifle towards the sunlight, allowing a tell-tale reflection from the lens. He considered that he was perhaps a novice, or had dug in early in the day and was not prepared to move his position. His opponent did not have appeared to have studied such renown snipers as the American Carlos Hatchcock, whose finest kill was shooting clean through an opponent's rifle sight from 500 yards after seeing a shimmer of reflecting sunlight. During a discussion about the incident his colleagues congratulated him on his marksmanship, with one jovially suggesting that it was a lucky shot that had hit one of the rocks that surrounded the hole and deflected into the sniper's skull. But, there were no such marks on the rocks that surrounded the gap to validate the theory. Although, even if that had been the case, Dutch would have had no concern, as all that mattered was that he had successfully completed his mission. He was very satisfied at the final outcome. Job done.

CHAPTER 13

Trouble *(2000)*

Artists: Coldplay
Writers: Berryman, Buckland, Champion, Martin

Dutch was taking a welcomed shower following a particularly tough hilly 10k training run, when he heard the 'Land of Hope and Glory' ring tone emanating from his mobile phone in the bedroom. Not willing to cut short the enjoyable experience of the cooling down from the tepid water for another possible unwanted contact from a call centre, he ignored the interruption.

Once dried and dressed he examined his mobile which indicated that the call had been from his sister Jeanette, and although they kept in telephone contact, she would only usually call if she had some particular news of interest to him.

Dutch returned her call, and both having exchanged general family chat, Jeanette went on to say:

"It's nice speaking to you Den, but I must be honest the main reason I am calling you is that I am extremely worried about Roy."

"What's different Sis, the whole family are constantly worried about our dear brother."

That's true, but it's a bit more serious this time, as he's been arrested yet again, but this time due to his ever-lengthening criminal record the courts are losing patience with him. Two weeks ago, he was sentenced to six months imprisonment suspended for two years. He's had all the fines and probation orders and conditional discharges, the only reason he didn't go down there and then was because his solicitor Tim Hunt arranged for me to address the court to let me confirm that he could live with me rather than in that hostel."

"That's great of you. Getting him out of that place will help, but there is no way you can nursemaid him for two years. Once he gets fed up at your place he will be straight back on the streets with his dodgy mates and the whole cycle will start again."

"Exactly Den, and that's why I needed to speak to you. He hasn't been outside my door since the case, but he's getting fed up now and is demanding his phone back which I have hidden to stop him getting any drugs, because that's the root of his problem."

"If he's been indoors and behaving himself for two weeks, I am guessing that he's still only using cannabis with the occasional coke when he can afford it, otherwise he would be going up the wall."

"Roy has really been trying. He's not clinically addicted, but as you know he suffers badly from depression and he sees drugs as a relief from his dark feelings. As you say it's a constant cycle. He can't get a job because of his convictions and has too much time on his hands to think, and sinks even deeper. So to get money for the stuff he commits minor crime."

"What sort of stuff has he been doing?"

"The usual crap, possession of cannabis and selling the stuff for people to earn a few pounds to buy his weed, or coke when he feels the need for it. As you know he's not really a bad person and has never been violent towards anyone, it's all about his anxiety and depression."

"Has he not been taking the anti- depression tablets prescribed by his doctor?"

"Yes, he has, but he says that are not helping, so I've actually got an appointment for me to go into the surgery with him and see his doctor tomorrow. But even if we get something different that helps, he's got no chance of staying on the straight and narrow if he stays in Brighton. He only knows the rough crowd."

"You are spot on there, but what's the solution?"

"I was wondering if another member of the family who lives a long way from Brighton could help, but although Deborah and Barry live far enough away they have still got some of their kids living with them. You and Melanie are in a similar position living with Molly and Ken, so there seems little hope for him, as I can't keep him in forever."

Dutch momentarily paused the conversation, and after a short period said," Take Roy to the doctors tomorrow as planned and make sure you tell the quack the whole story and insist that he tries another medication. After you get back from there, whatever you need to do keep Roy indoors until you hear from me. I have an idea and if it works out I will be with you within 48 hours. Tie the little bastard up if you have to, we must finally put a stop to this."

"Oh! thanks for that Den. I don't know if you are able to do anything for him but at least you have given me some hope. Neither of us want our brother to yo, yo in and out of prison because that's what's going to happen if he doesn't move on. If he did go inside his delicate mental condition would worsen"

"He's not really a bad person, he got himself in a rut when younger and can't find a way out of it. The trouble is that he will never ask for help, he's 48 now, still stumbling around in life with nothing of his own. He should have joined the army like me."

"Den, you must be joking. Roy in the army! He is much to gentle for that, the only person that he could ever manage to kill would be himself!"

"True. I think over the years the court have recognised his frailties, that's why he has avoided the threat of prison until now. It's such a shame that he hasn't been able to move on from all the shit that we experienced as youngsters. As you say he was no fighter, although he was older than me, I got into loads of fights trying to protect him, which either ended up in me getting beaten up, or in trouble if I came off best. I hope we can help him. If it wasn't for the army, there but for the grace of God go I."

"Thinking about it, it's surprising that after all the constant bullying and humiliation that we received as kids just because we were living on the poverty line, only one of the five has fallen by the wayside. I can still remember that awful day when a kid recognised that Roy and you were wearing his old clothes that his parents had given to the charity shop."

"Unfortunately, so can I, they really took the piss out of us which resulted in yet another scrap. It's no wonder I ended up fighting all my life, I had enough practice from a very early age!"

"Bless poor old nan and grand, they tried to do the best for us, but that was as much as they could afford."

"Yes, bless them both, they did all they could to keep us all together. Okay Sis, just keep Roy indoors and away from the phone and I'll try to organise something. I can't promise anything, but I will definitely be down soon to help, regardless of whether I've found a solution or not."

"Thanks Den, I'm so glad I called you, He will be so pleased to see you, I'm sure he will agree to stay indoors when I tell him you're coming down as he idolises you. Bye."

After a brief moment of thought Dutch located Melanie and related the problem to her. Melanie had only met Roy on a few occasions, and despite his wayward reputation she had always found him pleasant and respectful towards her. Dutch then relayed his thoughts about a possible solution to the problem of removing Roy from Brighton and the temptations that surrounded him.

Melanie had a few reservations, but was sympathetic as to why her husband would need to try to assist his brother in a time of crisis.

Having spoken to Melanie and gained her support he made a call to Ross.

"Hi Ross, its Dutch how are you diddling?"

"I'm okay mate. Where have you been, haven't seen you for a few weeks?"

"I just haven't had the time to get up to you lately. As I've not heard about any group activity, I guess all is quiet?"

"Yeah, not much happening. We've purposely not called on you anyway, as you have done more than your share in recent months. For what do I owe the pleasure of your call today?"

"Last time I saw you, you mentioned that your head steward and cook Keith, was leaving and you would be looking for a replacement. Have you filled the post yet?"

"Christ Dutch, is the tour business got that bad that you need another job?"

"No, it wouldn't be me applying, it would be my brother Roy."

"Well the position is still open I haven't advertised it yet. I was going to step in for a while until I found someone suitable. So, your brother would be interested in the job then?"

"I will be honest with you Ross; Roy doesn't even know about the job. He's forty-eight, homeless and still lives in Brighton. He's only ever had manual jobs and has a list of petty criminal offences, mainly due to his habit of smoking cannabis and keeping bad company. I need to get him out of Brighton away from all he has ever known, or he will soon end up in prison."

Ross paused for a moment, then said, "Well Dutch that's got to be the worse employment reference ever. I can't say that you have sold him to me! With respect Dutch, I'm finding your request really odd as you have spent so much of your own time successfully eradicating crime from this area, but now you are planning on importing a possible problem here!"

"I can obviously see why you would think like that, but if you met him, you would soon realise that underneath he is a good guy who deserves a break. His problems all stem from the circumstances of our early lives which have haunted him ever since, taking him down a path from which he's never managed to recover. I'm sure once Roy's out of his unstable environment, having regular employment and mixing with decent, honest folk he will soon settle down, and be no problem to anyone. What's more, he will have me on his back. Believe me he won't want to let me down. But if he does I will guarantee to reimburse you for any financial losses."

"As its you I'll give him a trial, as I also have an elder brother, and if he were in a similar position I would want to help him out. But If I do this Dutch, and he lets us both down I will get shot of him immediately, as like you I have a reputable business to run. As you know he would be handling cash, also some of the players leave valuables unattended, so he had better not get sticky fingers. You had also better warn him that I will not tolerate the use of any kind of drugs on my grounds, including cannabis, one whiff of anything and he'd be out. We also have health and safety to consider, and I will not tolerate anyone under the influence being around dangerous tools and weapons. I will certainly be having strong words with him before he starts, so he will know exactly where he stands, and I'm sure, by then you would have done the same."

"That's great news Ross. I realise that you are taking a risk, I can assure you he will be in no doubt from me as to what's expected of him. Roy has worked in different roles on numerous building sites in the past and is quite a handy person when he puts his mind to it. So I know he can do the job here, or I wouldn't have bothered you. If you want to put him on a probationary period, I will financial support him until you have decided whether or not he's proficient enough for you to employ on a wage."

"That seems fair enough, it will give us chance to have a good look at him and to see how we get on together. Is he going to be living with you and Mel?"

"I haven't yet figured that out yet as this has only just been sprung on me. I will probably have to convert the garage into some suitable accommodation a bit pronto."

"As we're both hopeful this all pans out well, he could take over the cabin up at the air soft site as Keith has already moved his stuff out. It has all he will need including a toilet and a shower."

"That's brilliant Ross. I'm so grateful, and I'm sure once he realises what a lucky break he has been given, he will be too. I'll make sure this works, or he'll be straight back down the road, as I can't let him disrupt our lives here if he can't behave himself."

"I know you well enough as a friend that you will do all in your power to both help your brother and to protect my business, so it's not that much of a risk for me to take. He can make a start when he's ready."

"I really appreciate that you feel that you can put your trust in me that way, and to give Roy his last chance to make a decent life for himself. I am in your debt once more mate!"

"You silly bugger, you owe me nothing, no one has done more recently to help our community than you. It's a two-way road you know."

"Cheers then Ross, it looks as if I'm on my way back down to Sussex for a few days."

Having informed Melanie of his immediate plans, Dutch carried out the following days' tours. During the intervals he made arrangements with another tour operator, with whom he had a reciprocal agreement to cover his next two days bookings.

As soon as he had completed his day's work, he kissed Melanie goodbye and commenced the lengthy journey to the south coast in her more economical saloon car.

CHAPTER 14

Handle with Care *(1988)*

Artists: Traveling Wilburys
Writers: Harrison, Lynne, Orbison, Petty, Dylan,

After a pleasant and uneventful five-hour run, Dutch was grateful to arrive at Jeanette's just before midnight, having been driving almost constantly since early morning.

The joyous reception that Dutch received from his brother and sister was emotional, with the three of them expressing regret that they had not made more of an effort in the past to keep more regular contact.

He was somewhat pleasantly surprised at Roy's appearance, as last time Dutch had been in his company, he had long unkempt hair and was scruffy. He was now well groomed and although he had a pale complexion he still looked about ten years younger than his age and without an ounce of fat on him. Dutch's cynical thoughts were that the new hair style and general improved appearance was probably brought about by his recent court appearance, and his slim looks were probably due to him purchasing drugs in favour of food. But, perhaps his negative thoughts were unfair, and his brother's improved image was because during the previous fortnight, having been well looked after by Jeanette he had finally decided to kick his bad habits in an attempt to turn his life around.

Following pleasant conversations over a late supper, Dutch got straight down to the point.

"Roy, I'm not purely here for a social visit. I have come with a proposition for you which I hope you find agreeable, because, if not, you will not only be letting yourself down, but also us."

"Oh, oh this sound a bit serious."

"It is bloody serious for you Roy, because you have a suspended sentence hanging over your head and once you leave this house you will soon return to your old ways and eventually prison. You know you are not the type to handle being banged up with hardened villains."

"Not necessarily-ask Jeanette, I've not been out for over two weeks and all I've had is fags and booze,"

That's brilliant Roy, but if Jeanette hadn't been keeping a constant eye on you, you would be with your so-called mates back on the wacky baccy, and God knows what else. I'm sure it's not been easy for you, but your stay here has proved you are not addicted to any drug, and can do without it, so how about permanently stopping and changing your lifestyle from now. Surely it's about time at your age to make a new start?"

"Ok, great, but how do you think I'm going to do that? I have no money and nowhere else to go apart from that shitty hostel. I can't expect Jeanette to keep me here forever.?"

"That's exactly what we want to do for you. I can get you a job and accommodation if you come back with me to

Cumbria the day after tomorrow, if you can assure me that you will change your ways?"

"Cumbria. I've hardly ever been the other side of the Thames. What's there for me?"

Dutch, frustrated with his brother's negative attitude responded in a raised voice: "A fucking better future for you there then what you have got going on here!"

"Calm down bro! You have sprung this on me a bit sudden like. I need to get my head around it."

"Look Roy, I'm sorry about getting frustrated, but I thought that you would be a bit more enthusiastic about this opportunity and jump at the chance. After all, as far as I know, apart from visiting Jeanette occasionally there nothing for you here except further trouble."

"You're probably right, but I have never lived anywhere else than this city, and you live at the other end of the fucking country."

"What difference does that make when you have no home or job, and all of your mates are low life. Think about it, how can moving up there make matters worse?"

"I do need to think about it."

"Roy, you haven't really got time to think about it. I have my own business to get back to, and, with or without you, I will be leaving in the next couple of days. To put it bluntly if you don't come back with me, despite your ripe old age you could still be some con's bitch when you do get banged up, which is inevitable if you stay here."

Sensing Roy's discomfort at Dutch's stern approach, Jeanette interrupted, "Den, please."

"Well, I'm only giving him the hard facts, he needs to wake himself up and take this final chance."

Jeanette calmly intervened again, "Listen to Den, Roy, he is making complete sense. It's been nice having you here for the past few weeks, but you, and I know that once you get back out there your troubles will begin again. Dutch is giving you a fantastic opportunity to turn your life around, don't mess this up. We're doing this because we care about you, otherwise we would just leave you to continue as you were."

"I suppose you are both right. Since you've encouraged me to stay in with just limited booze and fags it's been like detox, and I'm definitely feeling much better for it. Apart from you Sis, I have nothing to keep me here, so I will give it a go. What's the job Den?"

"You would be working in an activity centre way out in the countryside, well away from the kind of temptations here, and with one of the finest blokes that I have ever known. I'll fill you in on all of the details on the journey back. There will sure to be more than enough work to keep you busy and out of trouble. If it all works out I will get Jeanette up for a visit to watch you in action."

Jeanette quipped, "Roy back in work? That'll be a sight to see! No, honestly, I so hope this works out for you, and I can get up and see you both."

Conversation between them lasted well into the early hours, and once they decided to retire, Dutch, made himself comfortable on the couch, and covered by a duvet slept soundly for the remainder of the night.

As soon as they rose, seeing that the weather was fine, Dutch announced to both Jeanette and Roy that he was taking them out for the entire day at his expense, with the stipulation that to avoid any of Roy's associates that they wouldn't be travelling into the city.

Following breakfast Dutch informed his siblings that he was taking them on a guided tour in a similar manner to those he conducted in the Lake District, but they wouldn't be going far as he had another long journey the following day. As he drove he gave a humorous commentary on anything that took his interest, to which his two passengers found highly amusing.

The first stop on the tour was at the English Martyrs Catholic Church on the outskirts of Worthing. As Dutch pulled into the car park at the front of the church, both Jeanette and Roy expressed their surprise at the venue, failing to understand the purpose of their visit, as neither of them were particularly religious, and did not believe Dutch was either.

Having assured them both that they were not attending holy mass, he led them into the church and intently studied their faces as they entered. He was not disappointed with their reactions as they stared open mouthed at the wide expanse of ceiling above. Dutch had viewed it years before but for a long time had wished to return to see the spectacle.

As he looked above, the sight was as spectacular and colourful as he remembered, and he could see by his brother and sister's expressions that they were just as awe inspired as he had been when he first visited. In a whispered reverential tone Dutch explained that what they were viewing was the only known reproduction of the Sistine Chapel Ceiling in the world which had been painted by a local sign writer who had no formal training, following a pilgrimage to Rome in 1987.

Both Jeanette and Roy took photographs of various sections of the masterpiece but on viewing the images commented that pictures taken on a mobile phone could never capture the beauty of such wonderful artistry.

As the trio were about to leave the car park they were made aware as to the widespread reputation of the mural, as they noticed a packed coach drive in, displaying a Derby address.

The next destination of Dutch's surprise mini tour was the restaurant at the Brighton City Airport, situated on the outskirts of Shoreham. From the Art Nouveau terminal restaurant, situated at the side of the runway, the diners were able to view the fascinating arrivals and departures of private light aircraft and helicopters.

Roy made the comment that he wished that he had a light aircraft as he could then fly in shed loads of weed from Amsterdam, and knew of a suitable field on the North side of the South Downs suitable for landing it. Although Dutch had long considered that such practices must take place, he strongly advised his brother to keep such thoughts from Ross, until he had permanently secured the job.

Following light refreshment, Dutch drove the short distance to Shoreham town centre. Once parked he led his siblings across the glass panelled pedestrian bridge spanning the mouth of the river Adur. As they crossed, looking to the left was the commercial area of the harbour with its cargo handling warehouses beside the large expanse of costal water. To the right, the pedestrians eyes were immediately drawn to a hodgepodge of dozens of 'has been boats' restored and reimagined, all marooned by the high tide on the mudflats alongside the river.

As they slowly edged along the concrete path, besides what has been described as the wackiest houseboats in Britain, Dutch remained fascinated at the bizarre scene on his return visit. Neither Roy or Jeanette had been there since early childhood and were also both amazed and amused of how the owners of each craft had individually modelled their vessels.

As Roy and Jeanette viewed the floating homes and discussed the history notes which had been displayed by some of the owners, Dutch studied his brothers smiling face and excited demeanour. He did not see a depressed minor criminal but a man, now in the company of those that loved him. Dutch could envisage a decent future for his troubled brother. At the same time, hoping that the apparent new Roy was fuelled by optimism, and not just his newly prescribed medication.

After their inspection of the decrepit fleet, they all agreed that the highlights had been the 'home' that had been transformed into a WW11 bomber, complete with missiles, another which included a coach on top of a boat, and Del Boy's Reliant Robin protruding from a wall of another.

Following a lengthy beach walk to Shoreham Fort and well-deserved ice cream, the happy trio returned to their vehicle, when Dutch completed his finale by driving to Brighton Marina for their evening meal.

As they reached the tiny harbour with its bars, shops, and restaurants, whilst passing the on-site supermarket,

Dutch was reminded of his last visit to the site, when he had purchased provisions for the lakeside stake out which had successfully eliminated two pursuing gang members. He now had high hopes that such days would never be repeated.

After rising, the three family members ate breakfast together and happily discussed the previous days event, hosted by 'Lucky' of Lakeland tours.

After waiting for the city's rush hour traffic to reduce, Roy and Dutch said their fond farewells to Jeanette. As they entered their transport Dutch was surprised as to how little possessions were carried by his brother, feeling both pity and concern, that, as a result of poor decision making and low self- esteem, all Roy had to show for a turbulent lifestyle was the two bulging plastic shopping bags.

During the lengthy journey, the brothers conversed continuously regarding all matters under the sun.

Dutch was reticent when it got around to informing Roy regarding what was expected of him in his new employment, as he had held back some of the numerous jobs that would be required of him as a resident on the site.

Dutch had only got as far as explaining the cleaning and repair of the guns and archery equipment, arranging the cleaning of the combat suits, and the ordering and cooking the required refreshments, when Roy became concerned.

"Fuck me Den, you didn't tell me all this. You just said it was a job in an activity centre in the countryside, not all this shit that I know nothing about. Cooking for example. What the fuck do I know about cooking!"

"It's hardly cordon bleu. I'm sure that you have cooked burgers, bacon, sausages and chips before?"

"I've lived by myself for most of my life, so of course I have. Is that all there is to it?"

"That's about it, the only difference is that you will be supplying large groups."

"I'm really wondering if I can manage this?"

"Here we go again Roy, doubting yourself. That's always been your problem, you've never felt good enough. The last bloke managed alright, so I know you can do this or I wouldn't have put you forward. You are a practical person and can easily turn your hand to any outdoor work and a bit of simple cooking. Just believe in yourself and you'll be fine. It seems a lot to do, but you are not required to do all these jobs every day."

"Fair enough I will give it a go. As you were holding back some truth, so was I. One of the reasons that I agreed to come with you, is that I'm leaving some unpaid debt behind. Debt that I will never be in a position to pay back by legal means."

"Debt! what sort of debt, how much, who to?"

"Only about a grand. I already owed some to a dealer, then I got nicked with some stuff I had on tick, which also becomes my debt."

"A grand! Are you sure that you weren't dealing the stuff?"

"No, not really, that's not my style. I would always get a large amount for personal use and then shave a bit off to mates for a bit of profit."

"Fuck me Roy, that's still dealing whichever way you dress it up. Why didn't you tell me this before.?"

"Oh Yeah. I know you and what you think of such people Den, you ain't going to hand over any of your money to someone that you consider as shit on your shoe, and I haven't got any dough. I know how much you despise drug dealers, you would have probably threatened him, and if he didn't drop it you would have beaten the crap out of him. You might have got nicked and I'd be left in Brighton at their mercy. No thanks."

"What do you take me for Roy? Yes, I detest them, but I wouldn't have done that, I may have done some very stupid things in my life that put my freedom in jeopardy, but I had very good reasons for doing so. I certainly wouldn't risk jail for a low life dealer. I would have had to keep a very low profile, as I don't want the police re-visiting any of my old files. But I may have done something a bit more subtle. My main concern now, is can these fuckers connect you to Jeanette?"

"No chance. I've thought of that. There's no way that they know that she's my sister. If I thought that they did, I would have never left, I can assure you of that."

"That's reassuring at least, as the last thing we want is Jeanette getting hassle, or those shits chasing you up north, as I've only just resolved a similar problem- I hope!"

Dutch then continued to describe Roy's accommodation and the remainder of his jobs, which included driving Land Rovers.

Roy explained that he hadn't driven for years and would be a bit apprehensive of driving on the roads until he had some practice. He was reassured when Dutch told him that the vehicles were not roadworthy and used only on the private grounds.

Having discussed a suitable pause in their journey, they stopped at the Watford Gap motorway services for a half hour break.

Whilst eating, Roy said to Dutch in a sincere tone,

"I know that I haven't exactly jumped at this chance that you have arranged for me, but I'm really appreciative for what you are doing. You're quite right that it's my lack of self-belief that has always held me back, but not this time; I realise at my age there'll be no further chances. I'm going to give this a go bro, and try not to let either of us down."

"That's music to my ears, as I was wondering if you were truly on board or not. I guarantee that you can do all that is thrown at you. Just stay away from any form of illegal drug, no excessive drinking and be squeaky clean with money, as you will be regularly handing cash for ammunition and refreshments. Ross is a stickler for checking his stock and accounts, so will soon discover any discrepancies and any problems he will have you straight out of the door."

"Trust me Den you are now looking at a changed man."

"I hope so Roy, as this is your last chance saloon."

CHAPTER 15

He ain't Heavy, He's My Brother (1969)

Artists: The Hollies
Writers: Bobby Scott, Bob Russell

The freshly bonded brothers arrived in Ambleside at mid-afternoon, with Roy being immediately being re-united to Melanie, her parents, and the extremely excited Jodie. Due to a phone call received from Dutch earlier that morning, Melanie had cleared a space in the spare bedroom to accommodate a camp bed for their guest.

Following a discussion between Dutch, Melanie, and Roy, they agreed that Roy would stay in the couple's home until his permanent cabin residence was equipped to his satisfaction.

Before Dutch arranged the meeting between Roy and his prospective employer Ross, Dutch insisted that his brother took a trip to the barbers for a trim and a wet shave, which was followed by Dutch purchasing his brother a couple of sets of outdoor clothing and some sturdy work boots. Despite Dutch's feelings of trepidation regarding Roy's initial interview with Ross, his negative thoughts were soon dispelled when secretly listening to the proceedings from the other side of the office door. Roy who had only ever had a couple of official employment interviews in his life was rigidly sticking to their rehearsed presentation, and was showing a pleasant demeanour and an interest in the position offered.

The proceedings concluded with Ross offering Roy a three-month probationary period, but leaving the interviewee in no doubt whatsoever that his employment would be terminated at a drop of a hat should he transgress. At the conclusion of the interview Roy was introduced to his predecessor Keith, who had moved out of the permanent cabin accommodation to live with his girlfriend, before taking up a new employment. As Keith was leaving in a fortnight, Roy would have to learn and become competent at all of the numerous jobs very quickly.

During Roy's two weeks of intensive training, once Keith had finished his day's work, Dutch would familiarise his brother in all things concerning the handling, cleaning, and maintenance of all the weapons and ancillaries. Despite Roy's lack of experience in all of the tasks that he faced, Dutch saw how competent his brother could be at any task given the right support from genuinely caring people, a commodity not afforded to him in his past.

As the weeks passed Dutch was constantly monitoring the situation, and by and large was receiving encouraging feedback from Ross. Most of the few difficulties that had occurred were due to Roy's lack of experience in a particular field, but Ross was impressed at Roy's ability to learn quickly and adapt to a newly presented task.

To make his brother's accommodation as homely and comfortable as possible, Dutch was able to help both physically, and financially to equip the large wooden cabin to Roy's liking, and once complete he moved in permanently. As his new residence was out of town, and without transport, Roy was reliant on Dutch for the occasional trips to a pub, or to his brothers residence to sample Melanie's cooking.

Although constantly concerned regarding his brother's progress, the three months probationary period passed quickly for Dutch, who was wildly excited when Roy announced that Ross had confirmed his appointment and was now earning a regular legitimate wage, which was something that he had not done for a considerable time.

Dutch was obviously delighted that Roy now had money in his pocket, and that he was no longer required to subsidise his entire living. But Roy's ready access to cash gave him new concerns. As Dutch had been providing him with everything that he required over the trial period, he had been able to closely monitor Roy's finances, preventing him from being able to purchase cannabis or large quantities of alcohol should he have become tempted to return to his former habits.

With Roy's previous lack of money, and not having his own transport for the three-mile journey into the town, Dutch had been confident that he was behaving, but due to the change of circumstances, together with Roy considering buying a small motor bike or pedal cycle, new temptations would be open to him. The lengthy forced abstinence proved that as much as Roy must have missed the stimulants of drink and drugs, he was not clinically addicted to either, as he was functioning far better without them, which he readily admitted himself.

But, the situation would now need close monitoring to see how Roy would react, as like any town there was no shortage of the supply of alcohol or illicit drugs. It was imperative that Roy did not 'fall off the wagon' as the improvement in all aspects of his life were there for all to see.

Dutch put his concerns to Roy, and he sincerely assured his younger brother that he valued his new life far too much to relapse into his old idle existence. To add to Dutch's reassurance that he had changed his lifestyle for the better, Roy would often on his days off, ask Dutch if he had a spare seat on a tour, and if so, would join him and enjoy the sights and take in the information, just as any tourist would.

Roy became attached to Jodie, mentioning to Dutch that he would like a dog of his own as he got quite lonely living in the cabin in such a secluded location. That same day the brothers visited the Cumbrian Animal Rescue Centre, and later returned to Roy's home accompanied by a three-year-old springer spaniel named Ned. The new addition proved to be not only great company for Roy, but also new buddy for Jodie.

Life continued to go well for Roy, and Dutch took great pride when visiting the site himself, and seeing his brother completely immersed and enjoying his work.

The one serious error that Roy made in those early months was not at work, but one that many others had made before him, when underestimating the danger of the high peaked fells that surrounded them.

It was a misty Saturday evening, and darkness had begun to fall, when Dutch answered his phone, noting that Roy was the caller.

Dutch immediately recognised from the interrupted signal that it was going to be a difficult conversation.

He could hear Roy's voice fading in and out, and was forced to piece the staccato words together as best that he could.

The little of what he could understand of Roy's interrupted voice appeared panicked, Dutch became concerned and moved about the house and grounds in the hope of receiving a clearer reception. He eventually discovered a little better signal strength at the very end of his garden.

"Where on earth are you Roy? Neil Armstrong sent a clearer message from the bloody moon."

"May as well be on the fucking moon, as there is nothing else but rocks everywhere. We are half way down Scafell Pike and since the mist came down and it got dark we can't see a sodding thing. We can't make out the path anymore and I nearly walked over a ledge and have sprained my ankle. I was going to call the emergency services, but that will be embarrassing. What do you suggest as it's bloody freezing now?"

"What I suggest is that you get your head screwed on properly. What the fuck are you doing up there. You haven't got any knowledge of the fells whatsoever, yet you choose to climb the highest mountain in England. I know that you haven't got the appropriate clothing or footwear for that ascent, so it's no wonder you're cold. If you call out the mountain rescue they will not be impressed with your lack of preparation, which not only puts you, but also others in danger. Did you say we, who are you with?"

The signal again became intermittent but Dutch could make out the name Zoe.

The name Zoe immediately rang alarm bells for Dutch, as the only local woman he knew of that name was the driver of the van that delivered confectionary and soft drinks to the site. Dutch had occasionally spoken to her there, and found her to be a pleasant, intelligent character, but she was a throwback to the 1960's Hippie era, even wearing flowers on the headband around her long flowing hair, identical to many of the audience that he had seen in the musical film of the era Woodstock. On each occasion that he had seen her she had been wearing loose colourful clothing and sandals in all weather conditions. Dutch estimated that she was in her early forties and had always considered that she could be an attractive woman, but in his opinion had spoilt her looks by adding piercings to her ears, nose and tongue, accessories that he found unattractive. He had imagined that her clothes hid numerous tattoos.

She gave the impression that she was a free spirit and Dutch would not be at all surprised if she had been, or still was a regular user of cannabis, or other illegal drugs. Dutch, until that moment had no idea of their liaison. As far as Dutch knew his brother had only had a couple of female relationships in the past, and it had once crossed his mind that he may have been gay, but the most probable reason was his previous lack of confidence. If Roy were keen on Zoe he hoped his suspicions about her were unfounded, as Roy would always be susceptible to temptation.

During his brief thoughts, the phone reception faded once again, causing Dutch to repeat several times over,

"Roy can you hear me?"

Eventually Dutch received the weak reply,

"Yes, getting you now Den. I have had to stand on a big wooden box that's at the side of the path."

"A wooden box! Use your mobile torch to see what's written on the side of it."

Seconds later Roy replied," Stretcher Box 1 in large letters, and a disc below which says Rescue Post. Does that mean there are stretchers inside?"

"Exactly that, and if we don't get you off there soon you will be needing them as it is going to get extremely cold up there later, and I don't advise you to try and climb down yourselves. You said that you have hurt your ankle, if I came and got you are you able to walk okay?"

"Yeah, I will be alright, there's no way I'm coming off here on a stretcher, that's for sure, no matter how painful."

"How did you travel there?"

"In Zoe's van."

"Where did she park it?"

Dutch could faintly hear Roy asking his companion the question.

"At the National Trust car park by Wast Water. Do you know where that is?"

"Yes, I do, and I now know exactly where you are up there. I am perfectly capable of coming to guide you both down myself, but it is going to take me a few hours to get to you, so what I suggest is that to prevent getting hypothermia you both climb inside that stretcher box. People in distress have done that before and it worked. I don't know how well you two are acquainted, but as you will need to huddle together you may know each other a bit better when you emerge!"

"Just my luck that we have Ned with us, so there will be no opportunity for any hanky panky, it will be the devil's own job keeping him confined in there. Be as quick as you can Den, we are freezing cold and haven't eaten since breakfast, as we only thought it would take a few hours to get up there and back."

"You plonker Roy, it takes a reasonably fit, regular hill walker about six hours to do that."

"I just wanted to give it a go, as several recent visitors to the site have been talking about having scaled it, and asking me if I had done it."

"We will do it together sometime, but with the proper gear. Right get inside that container, and don't use the phone anymore because you need to save your battery in case you need it later. It is imperative that both of you just keep as warm as you can, and you will be alright. See you in a few hours."

Having terminated the call, Dutch explained the conversation to Melanie, who was anxiously standing nearby after realising that there was a cause for concern.

Dutch had once been a member of the local mountain rescue team and although he had attended the necessary training sessions, his actual real-life rescue experiences had been limited. He had been called out to assist on a number of occasions, but he had been unable to respond to most, due to having a mini-bus full of fare paying passengers.

On the two occasions that he had been available, he was amongst the team that had located a missing party lost on the fells and also rescued a climber who had fallen and broken his leg. He thoroughly enjoyed both experiences but had recently resigned, as he was concerned that due to his past unavailability he was letting the team down and they may have considered that he was not suitable for the role, which often required immediate response. So he decided to jump before he was pushed to allow a person with more availability to join the team. Although he was competent at the job he knew that it was the right decision, but felt disappointed as it was the only commitment that he had not been able to fulfil to the best of his ability during his entire life.

Dutch hurriedly changed into appropriate clothing and boots to suit the anticipated unfavourable conditions. He packed his old army Bergen with additional warm clothing, including hats and gloves, a towel, torches, a bottle of water and some various foodstuffs including two bars of the famous Kendal mint cake. Amongst the contents he included two packets containing thermal foil blankets that he had retained from his previous tours with the rescue team. With Roy's injured ankle in mind, he delved into his sports holdall and located a suitable elasticated ankle support. After grabbing a pouch of Jodie's dog food and two redundant army mess tins. He pulled on a black woollen beanie hat, and then tested a headtorch before strapping it around his head. Whilst he was preparing, Melanie had made a flask of hot tea, which she slid into a side pocket of the Bergen, together with some plastic cups.

Dutch commenced the twenty-six-mile journey to Wasdale Head in his tour bus, a familiar route having ferried walkers to the base of the 3,210-foot-high mountain in the past. Whilst he drove, he knew that what he was doing as an individual would be frowned upon by those involved in such rescues on the fells, and that he should know better, having once belonged to the organization. The reasons that he was taking this course of action was not only to prevent Roy the embarrassment of calling out the emergency services. The principal reason for his decision was that when the mountain rescue team attended an incident, invariably the police also arrived to obtain personal details of those involved, and the one thing that both Roy and the family did not need, was for the police to run their names through the police national computer and delve into Roy's previous convictions and any intelligence on Dutch's own suspected misdemeanours.

Dutch was sure that if such checks were carried out, the results would be forwarded to local officers, who would then view them with suspicion, subsequently giving them both unwanted police attention.

As he approached his destination he could see in the night sky that a low mist had formed over much of the fells. The only consolation that Dutch could think of, was at least Roy had opted to take the Wasdale route which was the easiest of the paths to climb the Pike. It was commonly known as the 'tourist route', but such a description was deceiving as the path became indistinct half way up and was often shrouded in mist, and still very dangerous for the unprepared hiker, such as his brother and Zoe.

On reaching the car park, Dutch noted that there were already cars and mini buses with occupants awaiting the dawn to test themselves against the tough terrain of the mountain. He was aware that many would be serious fell runners, there to scale the heights for training in preparation for the Bob Graham Round fell challenge, where contestants run, walk, or at the end of the route, crawl up forty-two of the Lake District fells in a twenty-four-hour period.

The extremely challenging event was named after Graham who in 1932 broke the 66-mile race record, over some of the most torturous terrain possible, including the journey up the heralded Scafell. Dutch loved his running, and had competed, and been successful in much shorter fell races, and had also achieved very fast times over the marathon distance, but he failed to see the enjoyment in such severe events, that could result in serious injuries, ending any further participation in the sport forever.

After parking, he made his way up the familiar slopes that he had climbed for pleasure, and when officially involved with a mountain rescue party.

Having walked along the edges of Wasdale lake and across two bridges, Dutch commenced the steep rocky climb, and estimated if all went well he could be with the couple in an hour. As he proceeded towards the stretcher box, the mist thickened and it was only due to his previous knowledge that he was able to keep to the track. Visibility was so poor that his headtorch was not sufficient to see through the damp mist, and a hand torch was required as a further aid. The adverse conditions and the plummeting temperature and thick mist, coupled with Roy's injured ankle confirmed to Dutch that

Roy had made the correct decision to call for assistance, as the many hazards were now hidden from sight.

As the stretcher box appeared, Dutch loudly called out his brother's name, as he didn't wish to surprise the couple, in case they were embraced in a compromising position. His call was answered by a bark, and as the lid of the box was slowly raised, Ned sprang out through the tiny opening, and excitedly ran to Dutch, jumped up, and rested his front paws on Dutch's thighs. A very cold looking Roy was the next to emerge, and once out, assisted a shivering Zoe onto the path.

The first words that Roy said was, "Please don't give me a lengthy bollocking Den. You really don't need to; we both know how stupid we've been. I didn't realise how tough it would be, and how long it would take. We should have started off earlier then we would have been back before it got dark and the mist came down."

"Lesson learnt then. You aren't the first, and won't be the last to come to grief on these fells. The local mountain rescue get over a hundred emergency call outs each year. Now how's that ankle? By the way hello Zoe, are you okay?"

Zoe confirmed that apart from being extremely cold she was uninjured. Dutch noticed that she was wearing warmer clothing than his brother, and was pleased to see that instead of her usual sandals, she was wearing sturdy Dr Marten boots, far more conducive to the terrain than Roy's trainers, which would have contributed to his injury. Before examining and strapping up Roy's sprained ankle, and confirming that no bones were broken, Dutch gave Zoe the opportunity to sort through the spare warm clothing from his Bergan. Once Roy was also more suitably attired in warmer garments, and both wrapped in the thermal blankets, all three of them sat on the stretcher box while Dutch served them with snacks and hot tea. Roy and Zoe were both surprised, and impressed when Dutch produced the two mess tins, filling them with water and dog food, which was swiftly devoured by the grateful Ned.

Once fully prepared to move off of the potentially treacherous slopes, the trio and their canine friend commenced the descent. The steep and slippery rocky terrain had a painful effect on Roy's injured ankle, making the downward journey very slow. It frustrated Dutch that the narrow and uneven path prevented him in assisting his distressed brother, other than going slightly ahead and clearing, or warning of hazards.

After making numerous stops to allow Roy to rest his ankle, they eventually reached the car park and their respective vehicles. They welcomed leaving the shroud of mist behind, affording them a clear return journey to their homes.

During the following morning Dutch telephoned Roy to enquire about his ankle injury. Roy assured him that apart from pain and swelling, he was confident that there was no lasting damage and he would be able to continue working the following day to complete a few of the more leisurely jobs. To prevent his embarrassment, he did not plan on telling Ross how he had so badly underestimated the climb. Dutch confirmed that he would not reveal his lack of preparation to the boss, who would be sure to give him some lengthy advice if he became aware.

Dutch then approached the tricky subject regarding his concerns about Roy's relationship with Zoe. To Dutch's surprise Roy did not become angry or defensive about him enquiring about such a personal subject, and in fact had been prepared for his brother to make comment and responded:

"I knew that once you discovered our friendship we would be having this conversation. I know that as soon as anyone claps eyes on Zoe they immediately form a certain opinion. From the flamboyant clothes that she wears, from her piercings and laid-back attitude to life she appears to be away with the fairies. Yes, she is different to other women of her age, and I know that she is stereotypical of a drugs user, and yes, she admits that she has used in the past, but believe me she ditched using years ago, and doesn't even smoke or drink anymore. She is just the person that I need around me, as she has been there, kicked it and will never relapse and she is determined that I won't either."

"It's not really my business Roy, but you can't help but see why I am concerned, as we have both invested blood, sweat and tears into getting you to this point in your life. It would be such a shame if it all went bent now."

I appreciate your concern bro, but believe me she is a good woman who works hard and most of all loves me despite all my faults and problems."

"So, is this a really serious relationship then?"

"It certainly is! I have even spoken to Ross to see if she could move in with me, then by her not having to pay rent we could perhaps eventually save for a place of her own."

"Don't take what I have said in the wrong way Roy, but I didn't know all of this. You've certainly kept it under your hat!"

"Yes, that's because I've been nervous about telling you, because I knew that you would be concerned."

"Good luck then mate. I hope that it all works out well for you both."

"I'm sure it will. The only thing we fall out is over the fact that she is a vegetarian and as you know I enjoy meat."

"If that's all you fall out about then you will be a lucky man."

Both chuckled, and at the conclusion of the call Dutch felt somewhat relieved and had high hopes for his brother's future.

Soon after the conversation, Zoe did move in with Roy, and the brothers did eventually climb to the very top of the Pike, this time with Roy wearing appropriate gear. The successful ascent enabled Roy to share both experiences, and give advice with confidence to others planning to conquer the peak.

Much later, following the brothers completing their challenge of conquering Scafell Pike a more bizarre rescue caught the attention of the mainstream media, as the injured party was not a human but a very large dog named Daisy.

The four year old 8st 9lb female St Bernard became exhausted whilst descending the mountain, with the weather deteriorating, and the dog's owners unable to move her, they decided it was necessary to call the Wasdale mountain rescue team for assistance.

The operation to remove the heavy St Bernard dog, originally bred to help with rescues in the Italian and Swiss alps, involved 16 team members, taking five hours to carry Daisy on a stretcher to the base of the summit, negotiating many obstacles including a waterfall on the way.

Following the rescue a spokesman was quoted, "Daisy feels a bit guilty and slightly embarrassed about letting down the image of her cousins bounding across the Alpine snows with small barrels of fortifying brandy around their necks."

When Dutch related the story to Roy, it made his brother feel much better about his original failure.

CHAPTER 16

Show Some Respect *(1984)*

Artists: **Tina Turner**
Writers: **Terry Britten & Sue Shifrin**

Due to public opinion amid a dramatic increase in the crime rate throughout the country, the government had allocated additional finances to local authorities to recruit more police officers to work within communities. Following the increase in manpower, Cumbria Police began to reintroduce the stationing of officers in rural towns, beginning with Ambleside and Brampton. Officers who were previously deployed from larger police stations in the county and travelled into rural areas, would now be based in the smaller towns.

This news was welcomed by all members of the 'defenders' group, who had first class knowledge of just how much local crime had risen since the reduction of officers some five years previously. This new policy would mean that PC Sleat, together with a handful of other officers would now be prominent in the community and should be in a position to react to the crime trends to which the group had previously and successfully responded.

As PC Sleat had previously suspected Ross of operating a form of clandestine activity, now that the officer was returning to his previous base, Ross could be under greater scrutiny.

After confirming the new policing policy, Ross called a meeting of the group. As pleasing as the new scheme was, there was a certain sadness within the group when Ross declared that they would no longer be operational. He explained that with more police in the community, not only should officers be in a position to tackle local crime, if the group's activities continued it would only be a matter of time before they were exposed, and, they could well damage a live police operation of which the group were unaware.

Ross explained that regardless of the disbandment, all previous members were still welcome to use the site during the same periods, the only difference being that they would now have to pay for the privilege. His statement was greeted with many jovial comments and complaints, but there was little doubt that the majority were pleased that all the activities were still available to them, which they privately considered very good value.

The defenders group may have been dissolved, but troublesome issues never fell far from Dutch's shadow. One such instance occurred when Jeanette visited her brother's Cumbrian home for a short holiday. During her stay, she and Melanie arranged to have a girls' night out in Kendal, whilst Dutch and Roy planned to meet with mutual friends in the local area.

Dutch had driven the girls to their destination, and despite his offer to collect them later in the evening, they had insisted that so as not to disrupt Dutch's night out they would return the sixteen miles by taxi.

During the evening, Dutch, a non-drinker, was feeling tired following a full day's driving, so he decided to call it a night and left Roy in the pub in company with others, fairly confident that his brother had curtailed his once heavy drinking habits. Once home he settled down to watch a film on TV, during which time Melanie and Jeanette returned. As soon as Dutch saw them both he could sense that there had been a problem, and was sure that Melanie's face showed signs that she had been crying.

Dutch addressed them both with concern, "What an earth is up with you two? I thought that you went out to enjoy yourselves, yet you come back looking really miserable."

Jeanette replied, "We had a bit of an issue at the taxi rank with some drunken or drugged up yobs, but we are okay, just a bit shaken up as to how vile one of them was towards us, for no reason whatsoever!"

"What! Tell me exactly what happened. Did he hurt you in anyway? Do you know who it was?"

Melanie responded to Dutch's vehement response, "Calm down Den. We don't know who he was and we never will, so forget any retaliation. We had just come out of a club and were first in the queue for the next cab, when three blokes just pushed in front of us. I objected and told them that we were next in line. Two of them were just silly drunk, but the mouthpiece of the group who was very slurred gave us an onslaught of abuse, saying some of the most horrible things to us. After I had given him a piece of my mind regarding his behaviour, he grabbed both of my arms and thrust his head forwards as if to give me a headbutt, but pulled away just short of my face. He then spent the next few minutes continuing to insult us in the presence of others in the queue, but nobody came forward to support us, probably because he was so aggressive."

Jeanette then intervened, "I tried to slap the bastard, but he moved out of the way, and then he aimed a punch at me, but was so pissed he nearly fell over, which caused him to pile on even more abuse towards us. Luckily, a taxi arrived and they got in, and for obvious reasons we didn't bother to object any further. Even as the cab drove off they continued to shout abuse at us through the open windows. I would have expected this in Brighton, but not up here!"

Melanie then added," How often do I go out, and when I do this happens!"

Dutch responded, "Christ! It's unbelievable that you can't both go out for the evening without hassle like that. I wish you'd let me pick you up as I suggested. Did you report it to the police?"

Jeanette replied," No, but we did discuss it as the name of the company was on the cab, and the police may have traced them from where they were dropped off. But we then thought that we would have to give our personal details, and you never know what checks the police would do, which could have opened a can of worms for you and Roy."

"I doubt if that would have happened, but you never know. I wish that I could get my hands on them. If you give me the name of the taxi company I could contact them myself. You never know, the cab driver may even know them, especially if they are regular customers or notorious in the area."

Melanie forcefully responded, "No Den, it's over now, leave it. You can't afford to get into trouble here as we have too much to lose. He will eventually get his comeuppance without your intervention."

Not wishing to worry Melanie further, and unable to think of a solution as how to avenge the upset caused to his wife and sister, he dropped the subject, but was seething inside.

Only a few weeks following the taxi rank incident Dutch decided to have a rare weekend away from work, and on the Saturday, together with Melanie visited Kendal for shopping. It was the first time that Melanie had returned to the town since the altercation, and unlike Dutch had largely pushed the matter to the back of her mind.

Having browsed the shops and purchased a few small items they decided to take a stroll beside the picturesque river Kent which ran through the nearby Gooseholme Park. The fine weather had attracted many others to the green open space, when Melanie suddenly appeared perplexed, causing Dutch to question her sudden discomfort, and the reason for hurrying her stride.

"What's up Mel. You were enjoying the walk, when all of a sudden you seem agitated and in a hurry?

Initially Melanie denied that she had a problem, but after Dutch's insistence she stopped and explained,

"If I told you I want you to promise me that you won't do anything stupid. You must mean it Den, or I won't tell you."

"What are you talking about. Why should I need to do anything? What's happened?"

"Promise me Den?"

"Okay, I promise, but don't understand."

"Don't look immediately, but those three that we have just passed are the ones that gave us the grief at the taxi rank."

Dutch immediately showed intense interest in her observation.

"How do you know it's definitely them?"

"I won't forget their faces in a hurry, especially the ringleader, who is the tall, skinny one with the skinhead haircut and the spider web tattooed on the side of his neck. I saw that clear enough when he grabbed me."

Not to show his interest to any observers, Dutch bent down as if to retie his shoe lace, but instead took the opportunity to survey the man that Melanie had described and saw that he was heavily tattooed on the left side of his neck.

On continuing to walk alongside Melanie, Dutch commented, "I did promise not to do anything stupid, and I won't, but I can't let this lie. You know me better than that. If you walk on towards that café and get yourself a drink, I will join you soon, and don't worry, I know that I can't afford to come to the attention of the local constabulary. I just want to figure something out to settle the score."

"Okay, but you have given me your word that there will be no violence, and don't be long, as just being in the same park as them makes me feel uncomfortable."

Once Melanie had left him, Dutch sat down on a bench far enough away from the youths so as not to alert them as to his interest in their activities. Feigning to be absorbed in his mobile phone, he was in fact intently watching the trio, who were sitting on a similar bench with their backs to a thick laurel hedge. Dutch had only been observing for a few minutes when his attention was drawn to two youths approaching those on the bench.

The pair went straight to the skinhead, and following a short conversation, one of the skinhead's cohorts furtively placed a hand through the broad leaves of the hedge behind him and retrieved an orange plastic shopping bag, which he handed to the apparent ringleader of the group. As equally alert as his associate for possible observers, the skinhead placed his hand into the bag and took out a small object, which he passed to one of his visitors, who immediately handed him something in return. The pair then walked off, and the bag was returned to the hedge by one of the remaining group. Not long after the obvious transaction, a lone youth approached the trio, and exactly the same procedure took place, with the dealers two accomplices again acting as lookouts.

Now certain that his suspicions were correct, Dutch left his seat and walked away from the area, only to locate one end of the long laurel hedge, which he followed until he estimated that he was immediately behind the apparent dealer and his friends.

Once he could hear them talking he crept quietly up to the hedge, and so as not to create suspicion amongst passers-by, he sat on the grass with his back to those on the other side. Dutch was able to hear nearly every word of their mostly inane conversation, which was regularly interrupted by further visitors and the rustling of the plastic bag, which although due to the dense thicket was not visible to Dutch, it was only a matter of feet away from him. It occurred to him to carefully reach through the hedge and take the bag and its likely unlawful contents, causing both loss and confusion amongst them, but he considered that it wouldn't be that simple, as they would be aware that the type of person that they serviced could also be tempted to do the same. What he overheard next caused him to consider a much better option.

He heard a more educated voice say, "Are you able to get me a 9 bar?"

He then heard a loud laugh and the voice of what he knew was that of the skinhead say, "Fuck me! I can but not now, that's not the sort of quantity I would normally bring here, but it can be arranged. How much are you wanting to pay for it?"

"Eight hundred tops"

You're joking mate! that's what I have to pay for it. As you're a regular, nine hundred. It's Paki black, and you can have it tomorrow."

"That's a bit steep isn't it?"

"Take it or leave it. Why a bar, are you having a party, or going into competition with me?"

"I'm moving miles to away to Uni, so won't know anyone who serves up, and will need some to last me until I find a new source, so I don't have much choice do I."

"Fair enough, but I bet you will divi some out and make a bit of dosh yourself. As you are a regular I'll do it, be here with the readies tomorrow afternoon and its yours."

The potential customer agreed to return to complete the deal during the following afternoon, and it became obvious to Dutch that he had left their company when he heard the skinhead say,

"That's a good result as I only paid six fifty for it, and its shit quality. He must be a mug thinking that I would only make a ton on it."

The comment which had caused the group great amusement, prompted Dutch to leave, as he had heard enough for him to have already hatched a satisfactory plan to satisfy his need for retribution.

As Dutch walked towards the café he felt both shocked and annoyed that a person who he already considered as low life scum, was not only openly supplying illegal drugs, but also making a small fortune doing so. He had never used an illegal drug in his life, but was aware that a 9 bar was a block of cannabis resin weighing 9 ounces, which was a popular way to bulk buy, as, if purchased at the right price, it could then be neatly cut into various sized deals making the buyer a substantial profit.

As he reached Melanie, who was sitting drinking a coffee, she pointed to her cup, got up and indicated that she was about to buy the same for her husband.

Dutch stopped her saying, "Don't worry, drink up, let's get out of here. I will explain all on the way to the car."

"Oh no! What have you done?"

"Nothing yet. I understand your concern as my past rash actions have caused all sorts of serious problems for you and your parents, but not this time. I'm going to use a much more measured approach to teach that punk a lesson."

Whilst walking back to the town on the opposite side of the park to where the three youths were ensconced, Dutch explained to Melanie all that he had seen and his exact plan for the following day.

Melanie, who still felt animosity towards her tormentor, gladly supported her husband's more passive method of gaining retribution then he had used in the past.

Dutch seldom took a weekend off work, so he was determined to spend as much time with Melanie as possible, which meant him rising early, preparing breakfast for her and Jodie and planning a long walk with them both on some of the more remote paths in the area.

As the weather was fine the pleasant trek lasted the entire morning. On their return home, Melanie together with her mother Molly, planned the family Sunday lunch, whilst Dutch readied himself for his return to the park. His plan included the use of his Burnaphone, that he and the majority of the defenders had possessed should they have had the need to call for police assistance, as he, like the other members involved never wished to be identified. He had diligently kept the phone charged, and used it occasionally, because if it remained dormant, it would be automatically removed from the network.

Dutch arrived at the venue a little earlier than the previous day, and as the trio were not yet present took the opportunity to fully familiarise himself with the immediate area and to take up a suitably concealed position. It concerned Dutch that a teenage couple were sitting petting on the bench where the dealing had taken place, which he considered may disrupt the anticipated proceedings. Only a short while later his fears diminished when the skinhead and his same two associates, without hesitation walked up to the couple, and although Dutch was not close enough to hear what was said, he could detect from body language that threats were being made for the couple to vacate the seat. It appeared that the seated male was ignoring any threats when Skinhead grabbed the youth's hoodie by the chest area and yanked him to his feet. It looked as if the lone youth was about to fight the trio, which again concerned Dutch, because he would not be able to see the youth take a beating without intervening himself, which in some way would be an ideal way to gain some retribution, but at the same time could also result in him coming into unwanted contact with the police, and would also not be the substantial punishment that he intended for his adversary.

Fortunately, the youth's girlfriend stepped into the fray, coaxing her partner away from the hostile situation, but even as the couple walked away they were bombarded with further threats and jeers from the baying trio.

What Dutch had just witnessed had made him more determined to see his plan through, as not only did he have an intense dislike for drug dealers but an even more passionate hatred of bullies.

The three then again took up their positions on the vacated bench, which prompted Skinhead to immediately retrieve the bulky orange shopping bag from inside the very expensive looking black leather bomber jacket that he was wearing. He then passed the bag to one of his accomplices who placed it in the hedge as before.

As it was obvious it was going to be business as usual, Dutch considered that he would have to put his plan into operation immediately, in the hope that his planned intervention would snare the rowdy dealer with the maximum amount of drugs, hopefully including a 9 bar.

Dutch then proceeded to use the Burnaphone to contact the local police office, the number of which was already preloaded into the mobile. Once in contact with the appropriate department he anonymously passed on all of what he had witnessed over the two days, and whilst making the call continued to observe the youths, giving the recipient of his call a short running commentary on their movements. Dutch was informed that they had no drug squad officers in the immediate area but would attempt to investigate his allegations. Dutch was disappointed at the reaction to his call and started to construct another way of trapping the prolific dealer. He came to the decision that if the police did not attend and get the result that he desired, he would attempt to follow the dealer to his home address, which he would then pass on to the police, who hopefully would eventually obtain a search warrant. Dutch was determined to disrupt the dealers operation in any form possible to gain revenge for his wife and sister.

Dutch continued to alternate his observations between the group and any possible police attendance in the park, and whilst doing so witnessed deals taking place, all of the time hoping that the customer for the 9 bar was not amongst them.

As the afternoon progressed the park became busy with Sunday afternoon visitors, many walking along the tarmac path situated between the trio and himself, when amongst the many pedestrians, Dutch's attention was drawn to a man he estimated to be in his mid-twenties, with short dark hair, strolling up the path close behind a young family who were approaching the group. Dutch had already suspected that the man looked like a policeman, and he became convinced when he saw his neat dark trousers and shiny boots. It appeared to Dutch that as the police were not in a position to dispatch plain clothes personnel, a uniform officer had donned his civvi jacket in an effort to reach the group unnoticed. He was obviously using the family to cover his approach from the view of the group. Dutch was curious as to how this one policeman could gain control over the three young villains, who would undoubtably take advantage of their superiority in numbers. But his concerns quickly diminished when he saw another man dressed almost identically, approaching the group in the opposite direction.

On turning his attention to the bench he noticed that the skinhead and both of his supposed lookouts were momentarily engaged in laughing and drinking beer. This had enabled the approaching men to gain some distance without detection, but all of sudden the skinhead spotted the advancing men, causing him to swiftly and furtively retrieve his bag from the hedgerow, conceal it under his jacket, and casually stroll away from his two colleagues.

One of the officers approached the two sitting on the bench, whilst the other hurriedly walked towards the departing skinhead. From his position Dutch heard the officer shout, "Police Officer. Stop where you are."

The verbal instruction caused the skinhead to change his brisk stride into a flat out sprint in a direction away from the officer, but towards an area where Dutch was located. On seeing this Dutch saw his opportunity to intervene and stepped out of his concealed position and stood immediately in front of the fleeing man, who attempted to run around him, but as he did so Dutch, with perfect timing, stuck out his leg, causing the skinhead to go crashing to the ground. Before the felled man had time to get fully to his feet Dutch pushed him back onto the ground, and as he held him down in a prone position, awaiting the imminent arrival of the pursuing officer, Dutch interrupted the threats and foul language directed towards him by whispering in his ear, "Shut the fuck up you little toe rag. Just want to let you know, this is for the ladies to whom you were disrespectful at the taxi rank."

The struggling and panting skinhead venomously replied, "What the fuck are you on about?"

At that moment, the officer arrived, and with Dutch's assistance placed the detainee in handcuffs. As he was assisted to his feet the orange plastic bag fell from under his coat, with much of its contents spilling on the ground. Amongst the small resin deals and small clear bags of pills, Dutch was ecstatic when he saw that the 9 bar wrapped in cling film was also present, and had to disguise his smile from the policeman. After gathering up the illicit items, the officer arrested the dealer for the possession of drugs with intent to supply. Having been cautioned the prisoner made no reply, only to shower a torrent of abuse towards Dutch, which caused the officer to say, "He doesn't like you very much does he. Are you the one that called it in?"

Dutch shrugging his shoulders responded, "I just happened to be in his path when I heard you shout, 'Stop Police', so I did my civic duty and stuck my foot out to prevent him getting away."

The officer thanked Dutch for his intervention and when other officers arrived to assist their colleague, Dutch not wishing to be called as a witness, took the opportunity to slope away unnoticed while the police were preoccupied with making arrests.

On his arrival home he conveyed the story of his afternoon exploits to Melanie, who immediately telephoned Jeanette at her home in Brighton, informing her of what they both agreed was a very satisfying outcome.

The following morning Dutch telephoned Marylynn the local neighbourhood watch coordinator who in the past had surreptitiously assisted the defenders group with additional information regarding local crime. Dutch told her of the circumstances surrounding the previous day's events, and asked if she could possibly research the incident and keep him informed of future proceedings. Impressed by Dutch's resolve, Marylynn agreed to flag up the arrest, and in time let him know the final outcome of the case.

It was many months later that Marylynn contacted Dutch, informing him that the subject Jason' Spider' Collins had been convicted of the possession of drugs with intent to supply, resulting in a substantial prison sentence. In addition, following his arrest the police searched the rented address of the unemployed Collins, and it became evident that through his lavish lifestyle, confirmed by photographs and travel tickets from regular exotic holidays, expensive jewellery, and designer clothing, that he was living on the distribution of illegal drugs. Due to this discovery the Cumbrian police economic crime unit carried out a thorough investigation, comparing Collins' assets to the huge discrepancy against his relatively meagre benefit payment, which allowed the specialist team to secure a court order under the proceeds of crime act to recover a large sum of his ill-gotten gains.

Dutch also learnt that Collins' two helpers had been released without charge, due to insufficient evidence, but never the less he was not overly disappointed, as although the accomplices had got off 'scot-free', they had not been the principal offenders that had caused Melanie's and Jeanettes distress.

When Dutch informed Melanie, she was not only delighted at the news of the conviction, but further pleased that for once her husband had controlled his emotions and had opted to act within the boundaries of the law, quipping that the world would be a safer place now that 'Spiderman' had finally met his match and was unable to cast his evil web in public for at least a couple of years.

CHAPTER 17

Every Day I Write the book *(1983)*

Written and performed by Elvis Costello

Dutch was one who continued to visit Ross and use all that was available within the secluded forest. As much as he had enjoyed his time with the group he was not sorry to now have more time for his work and other planned activities, one of which was at the top of his list.

Whilst working in Venezuela he had considered that his life story would make a good book from which a possible film could be developed, and since such thoughts, he had experienced even more riveting events.

His busy lifestyle and hobbies had never afforded him the time to ever consider sitting down for the lengthy period required to write a novel, but he considered that it was now time to put the idea to Melanie.

"Mel, you know that for a long time I have been thinking about writing a book, well I think that with some rare spare time on my hands, this is the ideal time to do it."

"That seems like an excellent idea. What sort of book are you planning on?"

"Crime fiction, but basically it will be on the lines of my life story."

"It would be a good way of using your time, but won't writing a book take a lot of research?"

"Not if I write it as a crime novel including all my experiences from both the army and in civi street, so I shouldn't have to use my imagination very much."

"I hope that you are not planning on including certain incidents that could link you to some real crimes, which might land you in serious trouble once again?"

"Mel, credit me with a bit of sense, it's not going to be a full bloody confession. I can change all the gory details enough so that nobody, not even the police who investigated me, would see the connection. Anyway, I will write it using a pseudonym."

"If you're sure that you will be able to disguise everything that you need to, then I think it would work. With all that's happened to you in life it should be a good read, but be careful you don't implicate yourself as I don't want to lose you. I sincerely hope you are not going to mention what happened to me in it?"

"I was going to describe something similar, as I need a serious occurrence to tip the main character over the edge, identical to what happened to us both. I promise that I will write it in such a way that even you will hardly associate yourself with it, but if you want me to use a different scenario I will?"

"I suppose if you can do that, it will be okay. Those horrific memories still haunt me, but I have learned to live with them."

Yes, you have done extremely well Mel. You know that I won't want to cause you any distress. It pains me to revisit some of those memories, but I'm just hoping to use this opportunity to write my memoirs in the guise of a crime fiction novel, but altering identities, circumstances, and locations of many of the incidents to such an extent, that for very obvious reasons I could never be personally connected to any specifically mentioned crimes. In addition, I would uniquely caption each chapter with a popular song title appertaining to its contents, so if the story were ever to be considered for a film I have even provided the director with some possible sound tracks."

Chuckling at his own flippant remark. He continued, "I have given this a lot of thought Mel, and I think I've got enough material for more than one book, and If so, I would like to dedicate each novel to some of those who have been important to me in my life, but are no longer with us."

Melanie responded, "You are determined to see this through and have obviously given it an awful lot of thought, so I won't waste my time trying to dissuade you. Just be careful what you reveal, as if you were connected to certain matters it could implicate both of us, and several others. I will back you all the way, as long as I can check it out before its published and you show your fictious wife in a favourable light!"

Dutch, smiled, reached out, and whilst holding Melanie's hand said, "Of course, I will, especially as I will probably be heavily reliant on your superior literary knowledge and computer skills."

"It will also give you the opportunity to let the world know about your intense dislike of bullying, and your belief that some amongst us are privileged of being blessed with nine lives. Do you know, from how you have described this book, I reckon that it could be ideal material for a Netflix series."

"See, you're getting the idea now, but I don't for one-minute think that any more than a few friends and relatives will ever read it. It's just something that I feel the urge to do, I can't even explain why."

Dutch was well aware of his limitations as a writer, as most of what he had composed in the past had been restricted to military reports, or contributions to website blogs. But, despite his lack of literary skills, he thought that he had an exceptional story to tell. Before commencing what he knew would be a difficult and extremely time-consuming engagement on his lap top, he meticulously planned the novel in both words and sketches in several notebooks. Once satisfied with his preparation, it became apparent that there was sufficient material for more than one standard paperback book of the crime fiction genre.

During his preparation, he was presented with ample material for use in his novel. Time and time again, whether or not he was searching for ways to disguise the true story of his past, something would always present itself. He considered that possibly the same person, or mystery being, that he believed had prolonged his life, was also responsible for the same valuable assistance. He would also be eternally grateful to both Google and Wikipedia when researching facts of subjects of which he had very little knowledge. Many of his inspirations would come to him at night, which made a pen and notepad essential, either at his bedside, at the side of his bath, or whilst running on his treadmill, as it was necessary for him to note any ideas before he forgot them.

Apart from the need to disguise the serious offences that he had committed in the past, he would also have to be sure not to implicate himself with the references to Kerry and her son Andy, of whom he may be the father, a fact of which Melanie had no knowledge. Their inclusion was a significant part of the storyline, and as risky as it was to include them, he felt to remove both was detrimental to the narrative. It would therefore be necessary for him to be prepared with a rehearsed deflection, should Melanie enquire about both characters.

During his preparation, for no apparent reason, with time on her hands, Melanie suggested that they complete a bucket list. As both of them were very happy with their lives, not including exotic holidays, fast cars or a luxurious home, the list was not extensive.

Only a few weeks following completion of the short list, he was to reconsider his options, as when reading an athletics magazine, he learnt that Andy was to compete in major marathons across the world. Ever since he had been alerted to the fact that Andy was possibly his son and was a prominent long distant runner, he had harboured the wish to see him in action, as he too had been a marathon runner.

At the time of publication it was not known what particular cities Andy would be competing in, so to ensure that Dutch was to see him run he suggested to Melanie that they attempt to spectate at the six largest and renowned marathons in the world, the 'Abbott World Marathon Majors'. The venues for such were Tokyo, Boston, London, Berlin, Chicago, and New York. Melanie was surprised as to his sudden desire to travel, which he had not mentioned when compiling the bucket list only weeks before, but knowing of her husband's love for the sport, and the unexpected opportunity to see some major cities, she gladly agreed to join Dutch in travelling to his desired destinations, in total ignorance of his reasons for the trips.

Before the commencement of his literary adventure, Dutch employed two local builders to convert his small detached garage, used solely as a storeroom, into an office for his writing, and for Melanie's hobby of making greeting cards.

Of course, he knew that his writing would not please everyone, there would always be a Vic Palmer who would feel it necessary to humiliate him just because they could. He was only too aware that if you put your head above the parapet there would always be someone there to try and shoot you down.

Once the office was operational, Dutch embarked on his long-standing ambition. At one stage, for inspiration he delved into his wooden box of the many military mementos that he had collected over his twenty-five years' service. He viewed his medals, the sprig from the pine tree that saved his life, and the shell case that once held the bullet that killed the rebel sniper. Then he ran his hand over the shoe lace around his neck, which still held his former identity tag and had indirectly saved his and colleagues' lives. Dutch realised that in the box alone, he had plenty of material to fill many of the pages of his planned novels.

As the first book progressed he found that although he had abundant exciting factual stories to tell, he did have to dig deep into his imagination to change many of the real circumstances, to prevent any readers identifying the actual incidents, or persons involved, which included not only himself but many of those close to him.

Having gone through the lengthy procedure of securing a publisher, his work was then proof read and its cover was designed to his requirements. Once the novel was finally published and released, the realisation that he was officially an author was a proud moment for someone who had not taken his education seriously, leaving schooling at the earliest opportunity, with very few worthwhile qualifications. He so wished that his parents and grandparents were alive to witness the event. The success and satisfaction of producing his first book fuelled his ambition to complete the sequel.

The completion and publication of his first two novels took much longer than he ever imagined, as general daily life had taken a heavy toll on any opportunity for writing.

This was to change, when in March 2020, to combat the spread of the Corona virus pandemic, the UK government ordered lockdown procedures that was to affect every person and every business countrywide. All tourism came to a standstill and the whole nation apart from key workers was instructed by law, with few exceptions to remain indoors. The economy of the Lake District was heavily reliant on tourism, so such restrictions caused great concern amongst businesses and inhabitants. Without work, Dutch grasped the opportunity to spend as much time as possible in composing his final novel. Having so much time on his hands he was to rely heavily on his treadmill, and the lockdown allowance of one session of exercise per day to expel his pent-up energy.

With little else to occupy his mind, Dutch found that from devising the narrative for his trilogy to its completion, dominated his life for almost a year. The few breaks that he afforded himself away from the laptop came after the lockdown rules were eased, but even when on the odd day out with Melanie and Jody, or whilst running, he couldn't break free of thoughts about the storyline that he was compiling.

Any nights that he remained continuously asleep for over four hours were rare, as he would often wake with the novel on his mind. Sometimes he regretted that he had entered into the world of writing, but it had now become an obsession that he knew would not leave him until this final story was told. Composing the books had also taken its toll on Melanie's patience, as the topic dominated their conversations, with Dutch continuously causing her frustration, by either asking her for assistance with spelling, despite having a dictionary and Google at hand. Dutch also had a habit of inadvertently pressing an incorrect key on the lap top and requesting Melanie's urgent assistance when she was either busy, or watching television.

The first novel and the sequel had taken him over five years, but due to not having work, or other distractions during the Covid crisis, his final book in the series had taken just a year to complete.

Soon after the release of the trilogy, Dutch visited his local book shop. As he reached the crime fiction section he immediately felt a sense of pride when he saw his editions displayed on the same shelf as books by prominent authors.

As he gazed at his three novels, despite their extensive alterations during production, they depicted many true stories of a lifetime of exciting adventures.

But, then whilst perusing he noticed a book titled 'How to grow old Gracefully'.

After plucking the book from the shelf and reading the synopsis he purchased the book, with the sincere intention of doing just as it said on the cover...........................

About the Author

Having lived and worked in Sussex all of his seventy years, this is his final novel in the 'Dennis Dutch French' trilogy. Married to Carla for forty-eight years, they have three children and four grandchildren. His hobbies include running, cycling, and listening to music.

His passion for writing a series of crime fiction novels derives from a long and varied police career and his admiration for our armed forces.

Lightning Source UK Ltd.
Milton Keynes UK
UKHW020731260521
384398UK00006B/192